WE LIKE BEING MARRIED
and Other Stories

Susan Harr

Published by Susan Harr
Publishing partner: Paragon Publishing, Rothersthorpe
First published 2017
© Susan Harr 2017
The rights of Susan Harr to be identified as the author of this work have been
asserted by her in accordance with the Copyright, Designs and Patents Act of
1988.

ISBN 978-1-78222-485-3

Book design, layout and production management by Into Print
www.intoprint.net
+44 (0)1604 832149

Printed and bound in UK and USA by Lightning Source

Contents

ABUELA

"ABUELA! MIRAME!"

Watch me, grandmother! See me. The old woman lifts her eyes, slowly, calmly, observes the little capering monkey figure on the narrow, powdery white wall. Careful, *nino*, careful.

"Abuela! Soy el campion!"

Indeed you are, child. You are the best one, the champion. And the closest to my heart. Of all my children's children, you are the most beautiful, the cleverest. Oh be careful, Cesar, do not slip!

"Abuela!"

The anguished sound echoes from the bleached, blank concrete. The child has fallen, yes, as she knew he would. These balancing acts bring their daily casualties as the little ones scramble up behind the big ones, richly brown limbs flashing in and out of sunshine and shadow. Laughter, shouts of triumph, shrieks of bravado turn to the insult of sudden pain.

"Nino! Vengame!"

The grandmother's shrivelled hand gestures, though her body, squarely seated, does not respond to the will, to the desire to run like a young woman, like a new mother, to the child's outraged call. Again she beckons, impatient with herself.

"Venga-aqui, Cesar!"

5

And the child trots to his grandmother, soldier-limp leg trailing mutely in the dust.

"*Abuela,* it hurts."

Tears, blood. Which flows the faster? The substances of this life, thinks the grandmother. It is what a woman's life is made of. Occasional laughter, but tears even in the joy of birth.

"Hush, little man! Tears are not for you. When men bleed, they do not cry."

But Cesar clambers knowingly onto the fusty, black knee, brings her his pain and dumps it there, buries his dark curls in the faintly smelly, soothing fabric of his grandmother's skirt. She smells strange, though he does not know of what. His nose wrinkles, but it is instinctive; with the prurience of a young animal he seeks her out, feeling neither distaste nor pleasure. This is just the scent of her.

"You did well, Cesar. You climbed higher than Marcos and better than Sandra, and more rapidly than Alexanders."

The boy snivels, his snot dampening the night-black linen. The grandmother raises the small angry face, and he feels the smoothness of her worn gold ring.

"Come and sit with grandma. You can help me feed the chickens in a while."

Cesar gathers himself more firmly into the broad lap with its perimeters of solid thigh and heavy stomach, enveloped and immersed in the warmth of her amid the cloudy garments and the resonant summer afternoon heat. Together they drowse through the siesta, too indulgent to go indoors, this little man and the old woman. For both, there is much to remember: for Cesar his moment of courage on that wavering passage along the wall, for the grandmother memories long kept, long savoured, her mind passing silently and with ease though the decades until she too is a child dancing on a sunlit wall, laughing from the branches of a high apple tree with all the ecstasy of those new to the world and unfamiliar with its ways.

"*Mamma!*"

Wide Maria, wide as her smile, draws a hand across her brow, wipes it on a checked apron, rests it on the back of her mother's chair.

"A cool drink for you both. Aren't you coming indoors? It's very hot. Ah, Cesar – so that's where you are. I thought you were playing with your cousins?"

Cesar stares up at his mother from his harbour of unconditional love which he is not about to forsake. Now to tell her that he fell? That he dirtied and tore his new cotton trousers, stained them with a warrior's blood? More work, his mother will scold, more work for your mamma. Don't you think I work hard enough all day in the shop and half the night too?

But out of the dark, soft haven beneath his grandmother's sagging breasts comes safe passage.

"The boy is looking after his grandmother, Maria. He is keeping me company for the siesta. What am I to do all afternoon, sitting staring at these mountains?"

And Cesar is further rewarded with a long drink of juice from his mother's shop. He looks at his wound with pride; dips his fingers deep into the tumbler and smears the sharp lemony liquid over the congealing scrape. Abuela wipes his smudged countenance with a tongue-moistened handkerchief and as the silken young face turns itself blind-eyed to hers she weeps silently, inwardly, the gladness and the tears like an offering for such a miracle, such perfection that has fallen into her family, into her broadened loins, her receptive lap, in the form of this exquisite, adored child.

7

The traffic on the terrible highway, running only a few metres from where they sit, menaces this grandmother and the golden child with its sharp braking squeals, its hundred-miles-an-hour discordant revving and the hysterical shriek of tyres turned too suddenly and too dangerously to cross the four-lane *carreterra*. Tourists and locals, they all travel fast on this road, speeding for the love of speed, hurtling through these quiet stretches to the next centre of civilisation with its flashing neon excitements: night club travel shop discotheque foreign exchange casino, new sex thrills, the brave new Spain and the new technological paradise, swiftly, precipitately, leaving behind anything that is yesterday's news. For those inside these gleaming road-rockets Abuela and Cesar are but a meaningless blur, a small black flicker in the corner of an eye, to be shaken out like a speck of grit from the motorway. Such sights are common in Spain. Who wants to slow down to have a look?

They built this road, years ago, to take the ever increasing coastal traffic, couldn't put it anywhere else as the dense granite mountains rise obstinately just behind the little town, leaving just a narrow strip of land to be relentlessly plundered; and the ceaseless movement to and from the urbanizations, the sprawling tourism that breathed life into a region that starved and went without shoes, hammers this ill-constructed route to death by the thousand every day with its unremitting din.

Carlos, Abuela's second son, is bitter.

"They have taken from us, and given us nothing," he will say after two or three cognacs in the bar. "They have ruined our coast, these developers, and what do we get out of it?"

"We sold our land for a good price," Maria's husband replies placidly. "We wouldn't have much to eat otherwise."

"*Anda!*" Carlos becomes irritable with statements like these. "We'd live – and we'd eat better than the rubbish they feed us nowadays. And we wouldn't have to breathe in the petrol fumes day and night."

"Still, we got a good price for the land." Alvaro remains unmoved. "The developer was very generous."

"Generous! *Hombre!* What a fool you are. How much do you imagine he's made out of it? And where has the money gone? Into English banks. German, Swiss banks, that's where. Not Spanish. Nothing is invested here. We still have high unemployment in Andalusia – so much for the tourists."

And so it goes on, the insoluble debate. The grandmother doesn't listen any more. The arguments, like the speeding automobiles, are to her just a blur of brilliant metal and clattering sound; she hardly hears or sees them now, but sits on her chair and looks to the quiet, still mountains above, where the rose and blue sky of dawn sends its cool sweetness to disperse the sultry warmth of the night and the sun fingers its way over those dense, magnetic peaks.

Later, she will sleep, in the hotter afternoons and then she will go to the orchard when the sun begins to ease its assault, wandering in the shade of the trees and calling to the fowl pecking in the long grass. This is the small parcel of land that remains to Maria and Alvaro. They have all forgotten to notice the concrete high-rise apartments of the urbanization that stand formlessly, with their blank uniform windows and their parallel balconies, where the land used to grow sugar cane and wild grasses to the sea. A mass of stone blocks and twisted wire is left, abandoned, where the shopping precinct, ambitiously started, ran out of money, and it is here that the children love to play, drawn to the ready-made adventure: not what the developer intended but giving delightful opportunities for sliding, rolling in and out of cement dust and the throwing of small pebbles. The children shall inherit the earth, thinks the grandmother as she watches them.

"*Abuela?*"

Cesar slides down from his grandmother's knee.

"Is it time to feed the chickens?"

Abuela nods. Without a word, they go to the back of the house, away from the motorway and its intrusive onslaught, and Cesar runs to fetch the bag of corn. The low sun filters between the broad, flat leaves of the fruit trees and turns the ripening pears and apples into food for the gods. Some have already fallen into the long, thick-bladed dry grass. The crop is ready for picking.

Maria's sister calls from the doorway.

"Mamma! Would you prepare some vegetables for us? If you are not too busy, that is."

The grandmother turns.

"Of course. I am just finishing here. Cesar will see to it that the birds are properly fed."

The curly head receives its blessing, the old hand lingering, trembling just a little. Importantly, the boy goes stiff-backed about his business, chiding the stupid birds that do not see the pellets dropped from his hasty young fingers, and Abuela returns to her chair at the front of the house, spreads that accommodating lap to receive the bowl and the parer.

"Thank you, mamma. It's such a help."

"*De nada.* The men will be home soon. Are you busy in the shop?"

Antonia's eyes darken. She frowns.

"Oh – as usual, mother. Much as usual."

But the grandmother knows. She sees the tourists from the urbanizations return with their bulging carrier bags announcing Hiper-Sol, the flashy supermarket five miles down the road. They only use the small family store for those things they have forgotten, or sometimes, one suspects, out of guilty conscience, or perhaps to fool themselves that they are living in the real Spain. It was good to have sold the land, muses Abuela; these people would never have brought us a living here. In that way, Carlos and Alvaro are both right.

The evening darkens quickly, without the preamble of an extended sunset, into night. Alvaro, Carlos and Felipe return from work. Grandmother's chair is carefully moved into the porch, and the family gather for the evening meal. The cheerful harsh chatter of Andaluz drowns out even the droning of the carreterra, and the meal is good. Cesar manages to get onto his grandmother's knee again, where she delights in feeding him off her own spoon like a baby; at ten o'clock he is too tired to eat more.

"The child is asleep!" exclaims Maria. "Mother, Alvaro will carry him to bed."

"No, no." Abuela shakes her head with vigour. "It is a shame to disturb him. Let him stay with me."

Shortly, the old white head nods too, child and grandmother asleep together, lifted gently and reverently to their beds by the men. Maria and her sister, and their older daughters, do the washing up whilst the men stroll out to the bar for a last cognac and a chance to argue further about the problems of modern Spain, the EU, Real Madrid's chances of winning the next World Cup and all the conundrums that life presents them with.

Tomorrow, it is the same. Always the same. The sun rises, the men go into town, the traffic passes in its monotonous cacophony and the grandmother's chair is placed in its warm spot on that noisy corner where she can see the world go by. Cesar conjures his usual excuse to sit on her knee, the children call to her, the chickens are fed, the shop does a little business and Abuela is asked courteously if she can spare the time to peel the potatoes or gather some fruit.

Today, the grandmother sees the English couple again. They don't have a car, these two, and so they totter along the edge of that perilous highway to the bus stop. Here she is, the woman, petite, with her over-bright silvery blond hair made so by sheer determination rather than nature, in a pair of tight-tight denim shorts and a low-slung cotton vest that do more to reveal her over-baked wrinkled, middle-aged skin than to promote desire in a man, one would have thought. Maria's husband eyes the woman askance. She looks like a gypsy and a street walker rolled into one. You see girls like that standing on the *carreterra*, thighs provocatively apart, waiting for the car that stops. But this woman has a husband, and he seems proud of his yellow and brown, shrivelled wife.

"*Hola!*" they cry cheerily with their bright, tourist smiles as they pass along to the bus stop. "*Como esta, senora?*" (carefully remembering to use the formal third person, Abuela notes).

The grandmother smiles, a more gradual, altogether different expression, replies in thick, rapid Andaluz. The couple blink and smile more enthusiastically.

"*Bueno, bueno!*" they exclaim as one.

Bueno? thinks Abuela. But I have just told them I have bad rheumatism today and I think the weather is going to turn.

The man peers forward through his heavy sunglasses.

We are going to Marbella. To do some shopping," he pronounces in his flat Birmingham Spanish. "My wife wants a new dress. She will spend all my money. I will be a poor man."

"*Bueno!*" replies the grandmother with a generous beam.

Puzzled, the couple retreat.

"I don't think she understood you."

"No, well, these old people, they only speak their own dialect, you see. Good Castillian is a bit lost on them."

"Nice old girl though – always smiles."

"Mm. Wonder she doesn't get bored out of her brain sitting there all day. It'd send me loco."

"Well, you're very active – for a man of your age."

"Cheeky, madam! Cheeky!"

And the husband puts his hand familiarly to the back of his wife's leathery legs and slides three fingers up the bum of her tight-tight shorts. The bus driver, observing this, shuts his automatic doors with a whoomph! and charges them extra. Besides, their Spanish is terrible.

A cloud of pale, sandy dust spews from the rear wheels of the caterpillar-bus as it heaves itself with caterpillar slowness out of the rough drainage ruts and onto the main carriageway, where it gathers speed; the grandmother takes out her linen handkerchief and wafts it in front of her face. It is already roasting today – the heat before the breaking, the heat that rises to the crescendo of a storm, sending mini-mirages rippling up from the road and melting the tarmac.

Her eldest son is visiting. He's done well, Andres. Works in a bank in Seville, a senior position, provides amply for his family. They have a good house, a big car and a good marriage. The grandmother looks with approval at Felicia, the daughter-in-law. She's about the same age as that English woman, but how differently she presents herself. An expensive silk flowered dress sits trim upon her full but well managed figure, and the black patent low heeled sandals gleam as though they had never touched the dusty ground. Felicia's sleek, dark hair is drawn back into a simple bow and her earrings are the best gold.

They sit, these two well to do Spaniards, with the Mercedes parked discreetly under the half-finished shopping arcade, near to Andres' parents' home. The grandchildren run back and forth, and are greeted by their aunt and uncle, presented with candies and trinkets. Cesar claims his usual place on the sacred knee, his dark eyes flashing a warning – *you may borrow Abuela for a while but she is mine.*

Knowing this, Andres ruffles the boy's hair and brings the gifts of a wise man – sweets and a toy car. Cesar grabs, grunts with delight, snatches them to his lair, trundling the car up and down his grandmother's compliant, sturdy leg.

"You're a lucky boy today, Cesar."

"Vroom! Vroom! You're a motor racing track, Abuela. See my car. Watch it crash."

The shiny little toy speeds off the broad, black knee and skids to the ground, overturns and scrapes along the concrete. Everyone laughs, and Cesar, ecstatic at the success of his trick, repeats the performance until the grandmother protests that soon her poor legs will be battered to ribbons.

"One more time, Abuela! Just once more!"

Vroom! Vroom! The car spins wildly into the air, double flips and lands dragging the ground, dust and fine pebbles spraying out in all directions. Cesar's eyes are shining; he claps his hands and shouts.

"They're all killed! Everyone is dead!"

"Oy, oy-oy!"

Andres picks up the excited child.

"Come on, *guapotito*, we'll get you an ice cream from the shop."

Felicia and the grandmother are left to talk, women's talk.

"And are you well, mother-in-law? How is your rheumatism these days?"

"I'm well enough, Felicia. The air is very good here and I like the summer. I think the mountains grow sweeter for me with each year that passes. I am very content."

"Is there anything you need? You know you have only to ask."

"Nothing, Felicia. There is nothing I need. Maria and Alvaro are very good. They see to everything."

"Yes. But – they struggle with the shop these days, don't they? Andres and I have been wondering – we'd like to help them. What do you think?"

"The time may come when they will need that. But not yet. We eat, we have a good house here. Don't worry about us, Felicia. In any case, my time on this earth can't be long now."

The daughter-in-law is genuinely shocked. Quickly her plump, neat hand covers the old veined one. The two plain gold rings lie together for a moment on the dull black skirt. The grandmother shakes her head with that long-ago vigour and purses her lips at Felicia.

"Don't look at me like that! I've lived a long time, and I have seen six of my eight children grow to marry and do well in the world. I have seen fourteen grandchildren born, and my life is still sweet, but the time will come when I cannot sit out here any more, or steady my hand to use the peeler or see clearly to feed the fowl. When God calls me, I shall be ready to go. There is nothing dreadful about that."

But Felicia does not like to think about death, about endings, only about pursuing and having more of what she has got, and so she sighs and says nothing. Andres returns with his nephew in his arms. Cesar is drowsy, sated with excitement, ice cream and an excess of love, and carefully he is replaced in his grandmother's lap to sleep with her in the long, mellow afternoon.

* * *

Abuela was right. Two days later the weather breaks and the thunder comes, and the rain that turns streams into torrents and rivers into floods. There is no more sitting out, and the chickens squawk protesting from their damp hutch. Only the English from the urbanization flaunt their umbrellas like defiant fingers thrust up at the brooding clouds, splashing past Maria's house to the bus-stop. They spy the grandmother standing in the doorway, peering through the fine rods of rain that drive like needles straight from sky to earth, and they wave in their quick, cheerful way.

"*Hola!*" mouths the husband. "*Que tiempo, senora?*"

"*Si. Mucha agua,*" says the grandmother.

"*Es como en Inglaterra!*" chirrups the wife, teetering through the swamp of the dirt track in her white sling backs. The see-through pink plastic mac reveals the cream mini-skirt underneath and the plunge-neck lime green sweater. Large silver whorls hang from her ears. Abuela knows nothing of England, and nods dubiously. Rain is rain. What else is there to say? It will pass.

Two days later, and she is installed once more on her old wooden chair, paring the vegetables and slicing the fruit. The children have gone down to the beach, older teenagers along with the young ones, running off their pent up energy after two days of imprisonment in the house. The ground is quite dried up and only the renewed freshness of the trees and flowers indicate that there has been a downpour. The air drifts down from the hills cooler than before, like light white wine on the tongue. Summer will soon give way to a sort of autumn, the slight change of season that Spain knows. Abuela creases her old nose, and sniffs. Indeed, life is still good.

16

The *carreterra* speeds up this morning. Frustrated villa residents leap into their metallic machines, baulked of their pleasures for forty-eight tedious, empty hours of switching channels on the satellite TV, captives of the weather that everyone forgets can happen here; dash from destination to destination like a trail of hungry, seeking ants on the highway. Under a cloudless sky they race for the glittering prizes: and those prizes gleam and beckon today in the brilliant new sun, like the inviting shimmer of the blue impossibly blue sea.

In places, the roads have cracked under the sudden strain of the torrent after weeks of parching heat, and some of the edges are crumbling away. Huge potholes have appeared and the surfaces are greasy with melted tar and the remaining water, mixed in an invisible, slimy film.

The grandmother notices these things and yet does not take any notice of them; familiar to her now as once were the quiet donkey-carts and ancient, lumbering buses, she no longer sees, but rather senses the wonderful cars, the hectic pace, the screaming road. There are potatoes to prepare, things to chop, Cesar to be watched; these are the important matters of life.

The driver in the dark green Aston Martin starts it all; it is definitely his fault, inciting others to race him like that. In a small corner of her mind, Abuela records this. The white Lamborghini behind is impatient; one can sense that too. Soon there are four vehicles vying for position on this impromptu race-track. And there – there is a low black limousine, stuck like a lozenge to the road in the outside lane, its hazards flashing as it waits to make the only right turn possible for many kilometres, in the forefront of three oncoming lanes of traffic and clear across three lanes in the opposite direction. The black limousine, distant, like a sandfly in the grandmother's vision, realises too late that the car behind him has not seen him; feebly accelerates further across the junction, swerves; but the Lamborghini hits him slightly askew at just over one hundred miles an hour, and then careers madly across the softening road, spins wildly into the air, overturns, double flips and lands dragging by its roof onto the road, a fine spray of dust and tarmac chips in its wake. It bounces into a ravine at the side, where the road has broken away, and richochets spectacularly into the concrete overpass some quarter of a mile beyond Maria's shop. Meanwhile, the limousine has been flicked into oncoming traffic; everyone brakes madly, feverishly, but there is a symphony of shattering glass, of splitting tearing metal, of cracking masonry and screeching rubber; and then a terrible, heart-stopping silence before an oil sump blows and a petrol tank explodes.

Abuela looks up; her hand pauses with the peeler. She knows that there was no time for screams, curses, prayers, recriminations: there rarely is. No time even for a last breath of that sweet, pure air. In a short while, all that will remain are burnt-out wrecks which smoulder and send off a sickening stench. It is the weekend, and there will be a wait before the police arrive, and then the coffins. These will house the bodies, and they will stay on the roadside until Monday, when they can get an official to deal with the matter. It is a sight that the grandmother has seen before, and the scratched film of fading memory plays itself out before her eyes.

People have come running out of the houses, the apartments, out of the shop; here is little Cesar, standing with his fingers in his mouth, awed by the racket. Then he turns and runs back to Abuela, clambering desperately to safety, spilling the bowl and the potatoes from her knee.

"Grandmother! They're all killed! Everyone is dead."

18

"Tch!" scolds Abuela. "Now look what you've done. It's nearly time for lunch, and your mother will be cross."

The grandmother picks up the scattered vegetables, restores them to her lap, and the hand that wields the peeler shakes only very slightly. Things go on. One must eat.

* * *

It is three weeks later that the grandmother herself knows that fleeting moment of finality, when the heart pumps its last beat and there isn't time for anything else you might like to do, for another look at the mountains or a walk in the gardens, a last embrace. It happens very peacefully, when she is having her siesta, in the warmth of the afternoon, just having eaten a little of the lunch she has helped to prepare. It is a death without drama, a quiet, dignified leaving of the world fitting for one so old as Abuela was.

A funeral for the grandmother is held a week later, at five o'clock, so that the sun is no longer blazing overhead but descending slowly to the hills. The English couple stand awkwardly in the street, waiting for the cortege; as a mark of respect, they would like to be there.

Here are her sons and daughters – Ana, Andres, Carlos, Maria, Luisa, Frederico – and the husbands and wives, the cousins and grandchildren; and then, it seems, most of the town as well. Pauline and Jimmy watch as the procession goes past in an endless flood, a flowing stream of humanity, behind the grandmother's coffin. The lowered sun is still warm, and the lively human river chatters, gesturing, even laughing.

Pauline puts a hand on her husband's arm.

"Have you ever seen so many people at a funeral?"

"They seem to be enjoying it, anyway."

19

"Yes, don't they! Not a bit like our solemn do's – more like a party."

"Look – those blokes are smoking! Seems a bit disrespectful to me."

"But have you ever seen so many people? The whole town's turned out."

And Pauline pulls self-consciously at the short, skimpy skirt, tries to cover a little of her sagging behind.

"Poor old bitch. Wasn't much of a life for her really was it? Stuck there on that chair every day. God, I hope I don't end up like that."

"No, well. Maybe it was the best way for her to go."

The English couple stand where they are in the street, a little at a loss, not liking to go further. The tail end of the broad procession passes, and the murmuring voices retreat.

Little Cesar stands between his mother and father. The cortege has reached the cemetery, high on the bare, sunlit hill, and the priest is already intoning the familiar Latin.

"In nomine patris…"

And in the name of the father, now the unmanly water flows down Cesar's young, brown cheeks, flows fast and unheeded, and the pain and the joy of grandmother are all blurred in his child's eye, are all blended with the sombre black suits of his father and uncles and the heavy black dresses of the women, so that what he sees is the shocking blood red of the flowers on the wreaths, the blood, and the pain, and the thankfulness which the priest reminds them they must feel at having been blessed with such a matriarch, all confused and fused into one sharp, indelible crimson image amongst the blackness, the infinite darkness of what is beyond.

20

A GOOD CATHOLIC WIFE

"CAMARERO!"

He summoned the waiter with the nonchalant ease of a man used to travelling, accustomed to dealing with service personnel in restaurants, high class stores, airports and the like the world over. Accustomed to being served, that is to say, as all men are.

The lithe boy slithered to Jeremy's table, dark silken lashes lowered in a shadowy crescent on the olive-skinned cheek. A handsome lad, thought Jeremy, perhaps popular with the gay clientele?

But Jeremy was not gay; far from it. In adolescence he had taken seamlessly to heterosexual activity, his first encounter at thirteen and a half with a girl a good deal older than himself – and she had made the running. In his twenties, his promiscuity waxed and waned, reached a peak, and then adapted itself to a few love-lorn passions for elegant and unattainable women who half-encouraged, half spurned him. Many of them, of course, were married.

He enjoyed the melancholy of these affairs immensely, choosing his love object carefully so that there would be no danger of a mutual level of passion, or not so much as to worry about. Affairs of the heart are always so much more stimulating and sweeter to reflect upon when things are just that little out of balance: when first one of the pair loves, wants more, and then the other, whilst at the same time no profound emotion is engaged. Or so Jeremy thought, having a temperament perfectly suited to unrequited love.

My life is very, very good, he said, when asked. *I have everything I could want.*

Then, quite unannounced, one spring in his thirty-third year – perhaps it was the onset of another decade, or a newly discovered, fearful tendency to spread just the merest shade round the middle after too many business lunches, who knows? – but around this time, an earthquake of emotion shook his world.

It was called Maria-Teresa, and she gate-crashed Jeremy's tidy schedule on the second day of his short holiday to southern Spain, striding through the Atlantic surf on the white, empty beaches in a spot far from the brash, noisy and altogether more British resorts to the Mediterranean side. As soon as he saw her, he knew the game was up. An arrow, surely aimed, pierced his heart, and found the one small place not protected by money, success or some amount of personal glory: Jeremy fell in love.

The young camarero beside his table rattled the tray, coughed discreetly.

"Ah – perdon!" said Jeremy, in his lamentably poor accent. "Vino blanco, per favor y – er – tapas."

"Claro, senor," said the boy, and then, rather deliberately, Jeremy thought, "y perdoneme," as he slid away.

Jeremy was left alone with his thoughts, which homed in on him with the persistence of summer flies and which were about as welcome.

Through what unkind twist of fate had business brought him here again? He did not altogether believe in Destiny, but it seemed that only some such malevolent influence could have drawn his firm's interests here, to this part of Spain, to the old city where Maria-Teresa lived. And where on his many previous visits, he had spent many hours with her. When everything in England seemed dark and chaotic, too much to bear, he would literally fly to Spain, with the sure instinct of a bird that migrates to a warmer, kinder climate, to the south... He would fling a few things in a bag and run to the airport, grabbing whatever standby he could – to Malaga and then hire car to Jerez, when he would drive at break neck speed down that terrible highway and up the next, and collapse, exhausted, into Maria-Teresa's welcoming arms.

In fact, such was the frequency of these escapes that the staff in the bucket shop, to which Jeremy dashed to claim a cancelled ticket or an unbooked seat, began to lay bets on when he would next appear.

"Here comes Desperate Dan," they said, as Jeremy's little whirlwind erupted once more into their computerised empire.

Jeremy would, of course, have been enormously offended had he known of the idle amusement he caused. He saw himself as a dark and Byronic figure, rushing through the night and the lonely, dawn hours to his love. (And dark and romantic he truly was – a couple of the bucket staff shop fantasised secretly – but even the most magnificent of us has our ridiculous side too, and the more cynical of the sharp-eyed travel clerks were quick to spot it.)

"Jerem-ee," Maria-Tersa would murmur, seeing only the handsome profile from where she stood. "You come often to me these days. Why do I not come to you in England?"

And Jeremy would redden, and fidget a little; he might be in love, he was definitely head over heels, but only in Spain. In halting Spanish, he would attempt to explain that it would all be spoiled that way.

"It would not be the same – " drawing her ripe, young, warm body closer to him - "The magic for us is here – " nuzzling his face in her waist-length, thick, rippling cloud of black hair – "England is not for you, mi querida – "

taking her smooth face in his hands and breathing the full sweet scent of her – "you would wither and die in our dismal climate."

Then he would sigh, a deeply mournful and passionate sigh, and gaze adoringly into her vivid dark eyes, whose depths he could never quite fathom; and Maria-Teresa would cry that he was right, that her Jeremy knew so much more than she, poor little Maria-Teresa, who had never been outside Spain, but she did want so much to be with him always, always...

Certainly, Jeremy was right. Maria-Teresa's beauty was of the brilliant South Mediterranean kind which fades and shrivels into misery under the cold damp skies of the northern part of the globe. Vivacious, intensely alive in mind and body, she would not be happy in the withdrawn, more distant way of life in England, and Jeremy spoke the truth when he said it.

Could he survive in Spain? Could he extend the Jeremy of the mini-breaks, of the stolen, secret days, the thrill of the yearned-for love, to fifty-two weeks of married life with a Spanish bride? This was a question he had answered in the negative, if only to himself, and it led to their last, violent quarrel.

"You do not love me!" cried Maria-Teresa, heavy tears soaking her huge, limpid eyes. "You come here only when it suits you! You never think of me and of what I want. I am beginning to – to – yes," she continued, breaking into Spanish, "I detest you! I loathe you!"

And she stamped her foot, not once, but twice, and shook her head so vehemently that the wild, rich hair flew amidst bold earrings and hair ornaments, knocking a wine glass to pieces and shattering Jeremy's newly-vulnerable heart in the same moment.

His command of the language was not extensive, but

it didn't take much to recognise words like "detesto" or "odio". These were terms he was not used to. He could cope with being hated; that was quite exciting, added a frisson, even. But these words implied contempt. A chilly feeling crept round his heart; for he truly did love Maria-Teresa. He had never felt so much for anyone, and he realised with a shock that even his little amusements and encounters in England had somehow all but petered out, and that there remained really only Maria-Teresa. He could not bear it if he became an object of her loathing. Quickly, he took her clenched hands in his.

"What is it you want, my darling?"

Maria-Teresa stared at him with the incredulity of one for whom life is simplified by abundant sun, space, freedom and wealthy parents.

"Oh, you fool!" she said, and her eyes welled with new sadness. "I want what every Catholic Spanish girl wants. To marry you, to have your children."

Jeremy bowed his head. He could say nothing in the face of this. That last word had set the knell of doom on any possible solution: children. A lot of them. Constantly arriving. Sleepless nights, nappies and all the repulsive things that came with them; later, a tribe of mutinous teenagers... No, there were no words.

"You see, Jeremy, I really do love you – as much as you say you love me."

Shamed by the simplicity of this, appalled by her naivete, he was yet humbled by it. If only it were so easy! He would not want to live with her here. She would not be the same Maria-Teresa, eternally pregnant; it would all be different. And how could he play the part of a contented Spanish husband?

"Senor."

He came back to the busy, thronged street, turned and

saw the young waiter at his elbow, chilled wine and a small plate of tapas proffered, now smilingly.

"Gracias. Er – cuanto, erm – cuantos Euros – "

"Nueve-cincuenta, senor."

Jeremy paid, and tipped over-well giving the pretty boy hopes that were not to be fulfilled. He returned to his musings, his memories.

On that last, awful occasion, it had come down to an ultimatum: he had had to back down. So, he returned to England alone, and the eighteen delicious, golden months of Maria-Teresa had been abruptly and cruelly snatched away, leaving him with but the dust of fragmented recollection and the echo of her voice as it screamed her final words which circled like vultures in his bruised mind.

Like a battered bird with a broken wing, he trailed back through the airports, unrecognised, unsung by the people in the bucket shop; like a defeated hero he limped back to his bijou service flat in central London, where he plunged himself into a despairing regime of work so killing that it cured him of all but an overwhelming desire to sleep at the end of the day. He made a great deal of money, gained a reputation as a hard man of business, achieved promotion with his firm, and made more money for himself. Of Maria-Teresa, he heard nothing.

And now, after all this time, two and a half years, sitting again in a cafe-bar in the once-so-familiar town, it seemed to Jeremy, as he sipped one chilled wine and then another, that this must have been intended, for good or ill. All the portents were there: his new company wishing to open up business in the region: "Someone with contacts in the Cadiz-Seville-Jerez area desirable", the brief went out, and the Spanish specialist they had called in struck down by a

mystery virus two days before he was due to fly, a hospi-
talisation case.

"Ah, um," Jeremy was obliged to reveal, this for the
sake of the company, "I do, as a matter of fact, know that
part of Spain quite well and I speak some Spanish."

"Well then," said the CEO, not convinced, perhaps, but
with no alternative, "you're our man in Espana in that
case."

It all quite definitely pointed to an omen. Perhaps, after
all, Fate was rooting for him; perhaps he was meant to see
Maria-Teresa again? Even – Jeremy's soul took wings – to
renew the relationship?

Confident upon this thought he rose, absent-minded-
ly tipped the handsome lad overly well once more, upon
which the boy had to be restrained from following him
down the street, and made rapidly for the nearest telephone kiosk; he did not want his mobile number to be revealed just yet.

"Diga?"

Maria-Teresa's mother – he would not forget that heavy
Andaluz, weary voice. Damn.

"Um – Maria-Teresa – er – esta alli?"

"Que no," replied the woman, discouragingly. "Quien
quiere hablar con ella?"

Jeremy sighed. Maria-Teresa's mother, on the slightest
acquaintance, had never liked him, distrusting this foreign
lover who came to take over her daughter from time to
time, and who seemed to have no firmness of intent. After
all this time, the barricade was unlikely to come down.

Patiently, Jeremy asked after her; after all the family,
the remotest relations, their health, their pampered small
dog – "Ah! Fluffy! La guapatita!" – and so on. To his surprise, during this conversation Maria-Teresa's mother began to warm to him, slowly at first, and eventually becom-

ing as nearly enthusiastic as you could say of the mother of a Catholic girl whom one had not married, but had in effect abandoned. At the very back of Jeremy's mind, in some shadowy recess, a faint warning bell told him that this was a little odd, that something was askew here; but the rising excitement he felt at being so near to Maria-Teresa dispensed with any such faint-hearted notions.

He asked where Maria-Teresa was – could he see her? There was a pause. He heard, clearly down the line, the indrawing of a long breath.

"Mi hija se caso... hace veinte-dos meses, mas o menos."

Married. The word fell like a heavy stone upon Henry's waiting ear. And only eight months after their agonised parting, as he was sure it had been for her as much as for him. It hadn't taken her long, then, had it? he thought bitterly. Suddenly he felt extraordinarily savage; grasped the telephone instrument as if he would like to have wrung the life out of its unresponsive plastic neck. He was more than in agony; he was a soul in despair.

But Senora Cebolla's next words offered deliverance. She assured him that her daughter would still want to see him; in the simplest Spanish possible, very slow, deliberate, she hinted strongly that the marriage was more or less one of convenience, a family matter, as after all, Maria-Teresa was getting close to the age when girls are no longer eminently marriageable (she was sure that Jeremy would understand).

"My daughter," she continued, breathily emotional, "still holds you in her heart. Of that I am sure."

Jeremy's hopes rose steadily with these protestations, rose with the precipitous ebullience of youthful erections, and as hard to push down. Perhaps it would be all right after all. Of course it would. He and Maria-Teresa could continue as before – well, certainly she was married, but that need not, if her mother's assertions were to be proved correct, stand in his way. Really, it could not be better, when he thought about it. He would avoid the necessity of a permanent commitment whilst continuing to enjoy the amatory pleasures of before. After all, they had got on very well like that and with Maria-Teresa's longing for marriage satisfied, their love making could be expected to flourish.

"Babies, though?" wondered Jeremy. "No, surely not. Senora Cebolla would certainly have mentioned it."

Quite why the lovely Maria-Teresa, so healthy, so obviously fertile, had not become pregnant in nearly two years of marriage he did not ask. Presumably – no, obviously, the 'convenient' marriage was not a very loving one. And there he stopped, unwilling to contemplate more, but ever hopeful that he would supply what Maria was undoubtedly missing. Without the babies.

Jubilant, Jeremy wrote down the telephone number the good Senora had provided, carefully noting the best times to ring: "Su mario... he goes away a lot... business..."

Nothing could have been better. He emerged from the kiosk a new man; the sounds of the narrow, congested streets of the old city greeted him, the cheerful staccato beep of horns, and in his happiness he blessed every last piping canary in its high cage on the small iron balconies above. In the heat of the early afternoon, he walked a little, watching the sun burn its way over the high, coppered domes, the antiquated buildings and the solemn, heavy churches; splashing the plazas, empty of children and adults at this siesta hour, with startling light; dipping behind the high roofs to the sea, bathing the ancient town with evening light and illuminating the honey skinned citizens with rosy gold as they emerged chattering, knitting, playing, drinking and generally living in the clusters of small squares and the dignified *pasarelas*. He felt at once very much part of all this, and of Spain, which was itself part of the whole, wonderful universe.

The first meeting, the reunion with Maria-Teresa, was as ardent as Henry could have hoped for; their second – after an interval – surpassed it, and after that, it was as if heaven had opened up its store a little early, purely for Jeremy's delight. Marriage had matured Maria-Teresa; there was a smooth, sophisticated gloss on the sensual beauty. Her manner, too, had changed; there was still the passion, certainly, the fire that in bed set sparks flying between them; still the childlike intensity that had so enchanted him. But there was also the sense of a woman who knew what she wanted more surely than before; and this reflected itself not only in their enhanced union but in her demand that Jeremy should make his visits to Jerez at times that suited her, according mostly, she averred, to her husband's fairly routine and predictable business commitments. This turned out to be once a month, sometimes twice; and on one occasion, he had to wait a month in between, at Maria-Teresa's request.

"Family things," she said, mysteriously. "A big wedding. After all, Jeremy, I am now a wife – a good, Catholic wife!"

This was accompanied by a little giggle, and Jeremy, with a delicious sigh of acceptance, feeling every moment a lucky, lucky man, allowed her to peel off his shirt and prepared to lie back and enjoy his extra-conjugal rights. If he had now to accede to a few duties, such as fitting in with a husband's schedule, why should he complain?

This unanticipated and blissful state of affairs continued for just over six months. Eight or nine visits had taken place, and on the most recent of these, Jeremy could not help but observe that Maria-Teresa seemed pale, rather tired, and just slightly lacking in her usual enthusiasm.

"Are you not well?" he asked tenderly, after a climax that was extra-sweet because of the uncharacteristically slow pace preceding it, a faint melancholy, even.

"Ah!" sighed Maria-Teresa. "Jeremy, my beloved... I am afraid that I am suffering."

"What?" Jeremy blinked. He sat up. "My love, my dearest one, are you sick?"

His love ran a languid finger down his spine.

"I am suffering," she declared, "from my conscience. Yes, Jeremy - " as he started incredulously – "it has caught up with me at last. I have not been able to sleep."

She paused, giving Jeremy the full benefit of her tired, somewhat sunken eyes. Then -

" I have had some sessions with the priest and – "

Her voice broke on a sob. Jeremy stared at her in dawning horror.

"And?"

"And he says, my darling – oh, my darling Jeremy, he says I must give you up."

"You *told* him about me?"

He leapt from the bed, glared at his manic reflection in the mirror. This could not be true. It was not real. Maria-Teresa was a twenty-first century, middle class Spanish wife, not a sixteenth century peasant.

"You – you didn't *name* me?" His words came through clenched teeth.

"Of course," Maria-Teresa replied primly, covering her full, prominent breasts with the satin sheet. "Jeremy, I told you, I am a good Catholic. And I am married. I go to confession, but the priest, he is sworn to discretion, of course." She paused. "I think you do not understand our ways. There are many such things go on, and if the priests were to tell, there would be many marriages broken! You do not need to fear my poor little revelations."

31

"I should bloody hope so." Jeremy's face was sombre, every part of him suddenly limp. "But as for giving me up – Maria, don't be ridiculous. Don't play silly games with me. I'm not into this whole idiotic, hypocritical Catholic set up!"

Maria-Teresa gazed at him mournfully.

"I know," she whispered. "That is the trouble."

Jeremy took her wrists firmly in his hands.

"Maria. Look at me. Look at me! I refuse to go along with this stupidity. Your husband is not being hurt. We love each other, you and I. There is no harm. I do not disturb your marriage – so let's forget all this nonsense."

"But my conscience." Maria-Teresa sighed heavily, even, thought Jeremy in an unwonted cynical flash in the midst of the trauma, a little histrionically. "It will not let me rest. Jeremy, I have really suffered."

Indeed, she looked unusually pale, her eyes not so brilliant, and there was a sense of dull strain about her face. He looked at her anxiously.

"My darling," he said at last, more gently, "we were made for each other. I will not give you up. I understand how you feel, but I will come again next month, as usual. The fifth, yes? In the meantime, please direct your thoughts to happier ends."

"Ah, Jeremy." Again that prolonged, emotional sigh. "You make it all so simple. But I am telling you – "

"And I am telling you, yes." His jaw tightened. Their eyes met, not in an embrace of love, but in a clash of wills. In Maria-Teresa's gaze Jeremy noticed once more that unexplained depth, the expression he could not begin to describe. A strange chill ran down his spine, a wave of such sadness as he had never felt in his life.

"Very well," said Maria-Teresa, after a moment. "As you will, my dear Jeremy, just as you will. So be it."

Satisfied, Jeremy let her go. His common sense, his rational outlook, presented so selflessly on the altar of their love, had triumphed. His will had prevailed, and with it the sensible order of the modern, enlightened world. With time, and care, he would wean her away from these superstitious beliefs. No doubt it was merely the effect of her new marriage; from what he understood, the husband was a good few years older and very orthodox in his views. These were factors that could not withstand the competition of a younger, virile man; namely, himself. Jeremy left that night in an unusually buoyant mood.

On the day arranged, he returned. At the airport, his usual, regularly-booked car was waiting; and if the car hire man greeted him a little more effusively than usual, and shook his hand a little more warmly and for longer, he did not remark it. It was a beautiful day even by Spanish standards, and Jeremy revved the 2500 GT engine with a feeling of intense pleasure, even sexual in its thrust. A nice day for a jaunt, he decided, and took the car fast around the roads from the Gibraltar frontier, through crowded Algeciras, where he stopped for lunch, onto the scenic route to Tarifa and then towards the flat marshlands where the mountains gracefully recede and give way to green plains and fields of sunflowers, and where the white towns and cortijas shine and dazzle in the clear blue light. Suddenly, Jeremy had an urge to visit again the place where had first met Maria-Teresa; he had a few hours before she was free to meet him and he was feeling particularly content and sentimental on this glorious, cloudless day.

The road to Zahara de los Atunos sang with a million scents and sounds of the early Spanish summer, the tarmac rough, uneven and hot. Jeremy accelerated; he knew the road well, and exerted his power over it. The snaking bend just before the narrow river appeared ahead. He pumped the accelerator again; put his foot down to brake hard and sharp into the double curve in a racing driver's attack.

* * *

"More coffee, my love?"

Maria-Teresa gestured towards her husband's cup. The already-powerful sun streamed into their pleasant, modern kitchen with its English-style breakfast bar and pretty curtains.

Raoul lifted his head from "El Pais" and smiled at her, his warm, brown face mellow with familiar affection.

"You make such good coffee, Maria-Teresa," he said. "How can I refuse?"

His wife smiled in return, filled his cup, waited until he had drunk a little, leaned towards him and said, so softly that he almost had to strain to hear,

"I went to see the doctor for my second visit yesterday."

Raoul stared into her face, with its tell-tale signs of purplish shadows under the eyes, the faint, sickly pallor under the olive skin. He raised his eyebrows.

"He confirms that I am about ten weeks pregnant."

Her husband breathed out, a long exhalation and his face relaxed into a wide, joyful smile.

"At last! Maria-Teresa, at last."

Maria-Teresa nodded, and began to clear the breakfast table. As she passed her husband's chair, she put her hand very tenderly on his shoulder, and pressed her lips briefly to his neck.

"By the way," murmured Raoul, rustling his newspaper, "have you seen this?"

He indicated an inside report, rather short, with a gruesome picture of a crashed car being dragged out of a local river.

BRITISH BUSINESSMAN KILLED IN FREAK ACCIDENT, the headline ran, and then the sub-heading: **Faulty brake cable to blame?** A small passport style photo accompanied the article.

"Dreadful, isn't it?" said Raoul, refolding the paper.

Maria-Teresa's face did not alter. Only the smallest flicker in those deep eyes betrayed any change of expression, a minimal increase in the rate of her breathing.

"These English," she said, lightly. "When they come to Spain, they are always so reckless, no? No doubt he was going much too fast for his own good."

"Indeed, my love, much, much too fast," replied her husband. "And now, do you think I could go and ring our mothers, and tell them our happy news, my good Catholic wife?"

A TOUCH OF CHRIST

THE BOY WOULD hang around the entrance to Sidi's hotel, loitering on the wide boulevard in front of the downstairs cafe and charming passers-by with his wide, flashing smile that put on show the immaculate, dazzling teeth.

Sidi was not charmed, however. He disliked street urchins near his place; the Muslim in him felt obliged to give to the poor, the businessman in Sidi felt the urge to kick the boy in the seat of his pants.

Samir was as hard to get rid of as the ants and the vermin. You could chase him off, on the end of a wooden broom, and he would scamper away with salaams and apologies, but an hour later he would be back, the white teeth irresistible.

When Samir smiled, he put his whole being into it. His entire countenance assumed the look of a cherubim; the eyes – large, dark, with their long lashes – would shine out of this angel's face clear and innocent; his healthy cheeks would glow at you, and his mouth, ever-mobile, well, it was hard to decide whether it was prettier open or closed. One forgot the smudgy dirt, the faint odour that clung round the boy, the torn, felted up sweater and the bare feet; the face, in Samir, was everything.

"Drat the boy!" Sidi's manager-receptionist would mutter as he rattled the keys, hurrying late stragglers to their rooms. There was Samir, still eagerly smiling, and it was nearly ten o'clock at night. "Have you no home to go to?"

But Samir would smile more widely and nod his head and then, laughing, shake it.

"Here is my home, sir."

A little bow, the hands pressed together.

"Oh no it isn't! Now clear off – and don't come back."

And Samir would retreat into the shadowy back streets, melt into the mass of tangled alleys of the medina, where he would be swallowed up until morning. Where he slept, Sidi did not know and was not disposed to find out.

The western tourists liked Sidi's hotel. It was right in the centre of the city, on the edge of both the new and the old quarters. The best of both worlds – souks and casinos – was equally convenient. The hotel was very clean and well furnished, in traditional style, it was reasonably priced and the coffee was excellent. Sidi did not intend that a beggar boy should spoil this image.

But the western visitors – if they did not follow the general policy of the hard hearted guide books and ignore Samir – found him attractive, a safe target for their compassion over the darker, abject side of Morocco that the hotel so efficiently protected them from.

"Poor little soul!" they would murmur, hands straying to pat the frizzy head delicately. (You can't catch anything that way, can you?) "Look at his lovely young face. And he always seems so bloody *happy*."

It was true; Samir did appear almost to be blighted with a sort of permanent, all pervading cheerfulness of spirit. Even when chided, threatened with a beating, even in the occasional thundery downpour he would stand ground, that smile breaking up the round cheeks at the slightest hint of approval, the sight of a pretty lady tourist, or the gift of a few centimes. A whole dirum, or two, would produce the most ecstatic beams, many an obeisance and choking, guttural Arabic blessings.

He did not have the usual, sullen faces of the beggar boys along the parade who also sold sweets; and he did not pull their tricks either. They would promise you –

let's see, holding up their fingers very quickly, is it eight wrapped mints for a dirum? – and then you'd ask for two dirums'-worth and find you only had twelve sweets in the handful dumped hastily in your palm.

"Hey," you'd say. "You told me eight for one dirum. That means – "

And then would follow an argument too tedious to be pursued and you would look mournfully at your dozen sweets and accept defeat.

Samir played no such underhand games. He simply stood there, one of the number of the wretched poor of the earth, ragged, filthy, and with that angel's face shining through it all.

"He's not quite right in the head," said some. "He can't be happy – not if he's a brain to think with, not living as he does. Hand to mouth, or what?"

But another, English lady traveller, on holiday with her daughter, murmured different things.

"He has a touch of Christ about him," she said, "this child. He may be – our testing ground. Amidst such poverty, he shows us how to be."

"Oh really, Ma!" The daughter protested. Her mother was undoubtedly succumbing to the religious bug so common in later age or, heaven forbid, early dementia, when the persona would be given to hitherto uncharacteristic moralising sentiments. The daughter thought dolefully of prolonged periods of dependence, of homes, of senility; and the prospects around her dimmed. Her mother, however, secure and untroubled in her increasing eccentricity, observed Samir with the detached calm of late middle age. She enjoyed what he offered.

"In return for pence, or fractions of pence," she concluded, "he gives himself."

Threadbare, in a pair of unwashed pants too short in

the leg and having many holes, apparently without companions or family, Samir stood in front of you and offered what he had, without reserve: the diamond smile, the radiating happiness, the sheer good nature.

"It is, you must admit, rather beautiful," said the English lady and Beatrice's snort of derision went unheeded.

There were others in the hotel who found Samir charming. A couple came on Judith and her daughter's third day there. Clearly they were frequent guests – Sidi and his under manager greeted them as old friends, came to sit at their table after the continental breakfast, talked of many things: of life, the world and its ways.

One morning, Judith noticed that the boy, Samir, was standing by the table of this new couple. This was inside the hotel, in its high-ceilinged dining room where the fans whirled tirelessly to dispense with any troublesome insect, the coffee came in tall pewter percolators, piping hot, and the croissants dissolved in the mouth. These guests, Judith reflected, must have great kudos, or Samir would surely have had his neck wrung. He dwelt upon the man's face with an expression of almost saintly adoration, standing quite still, unsmiling now, as if even that small muscular movement would disturb the object of his reverence. He did not look at the man's wife, who leaned back in her chair and remained passive, expressionless throughout this encounter.

Judith watched, and was moved. The man laid his large, pale hand over that of the boy, and smiled at him. Samir was being asked to sit down, was being served hot chocolate and bread by a waiter clearly repulsed by this whole, unnatural business of a beggar boy in the dining room, and whose nose twitched in exaggerated fashion as he leaned over Samir to place the victuals before him.

Samir ate ravenously, greedily, ungracefully, drank in big slurping gulps and then, sated, wiped his mouth on the sleeve of his decrepit, shrunken green sweater and looked up at the man.

"Good boy, Samir." The words were spoken with emphasis, so that the boy, like an eager puppy, would sense the tone if he did not understand the language. "Good boy, now let's talk."

His wife laughed, but it was a bitter sound, sour on the ear.

"Hugh, he can't understand English! What's the point?"

"He will learn this way." The man turned his big, pallid face to her and smiled. "That, and feeding him, is all we can do."

"Oh you and your *charity*! Yes, right."

Her husband shrugged, turned half away from her, and put a fleshy hand on Samir's arm to reassure the boy that all was well. There seemed nothing more to say.

This was repeated on the next three days. Each time that the manager felt that the boy had been indulged enough he – or Sidi himself – would come and sweep Samir out of the hotel, with the sort of clucking and *tssking* one would use to drive out recalcitrant fowl. But they were not unkind to him.

Once Sidi came to the couple's table, and tried to look severe.

"You will lead him to expect this all the time."

"No, I don't think so." The man looked calmly at Sidi. "Samir accepts – that's what so marvellous about him. He accepts what his life is, from day to day. He knows quite well that we shall not always be here."

"Very well." Sidi spread out his hands. The Englishman was the sort of customer he liked, spending freely and not questioning prices, and besides, he was buying an extra breakfast every day. "But I would ask you not to encourage him too much."

A nod from the big, broad-jowled head with its flop of light sandy hair; a lowering of the pale lids over the light blue eyes.

"I understand."

* * *

It was hot that day; Marrakech was preparing herself for the boil, and inland the temperatures rose and the plains steamed and shimmered. Only the high, distant mountains glittered with their capping of snow, like a backdrop of crumpled tinfoil in the sun.

Judith and her daughter took an early walk round the bazaars; they were going to escape to the cooler hills later that day, stay a night or too, and return to the Hotel Sidi Abdullah at the end of the week. As they were making their way back, a small figure darted across the crowded square towards them. Samir.

With his inimitable smile, he indicated that he had something for Judith, and into her hand he pushed a cheap, yellow disposable cigarette lighter, still with fuel. Automatically Judith reached for her loose change, fished out a few centimes. Vigorously, Samir shook his head and backed away.

"La, la-ah," he said, and made Judith understand it was a gift. No return was required.

She was touched by this gesture. Probably the lighter had been stolen – or no, perhaps better, found in the street. But still, he could have sold it and he chose to give it.

"Christ-like," she said again. "You see? It is what Our Lord would have done – given all that he had, when he could have taken, when he himself had nothing."

"Oh for Pete's sake!" Beatrice, exasperated by heat, crowds, harassment, flies and her mother, was out of patience. "Anyway, you don't even smoke."

"No, I don't," said her mother, smiling lightly. "So I shall be able to keep it for ever."

Putting her hands together and smiling at Samir, she thanked him in Arabic – this much she could manage. Solemnly, the child bowed, and ran away.

After the trip to the hills, they returned late one evening, the mother and the daughter, to find Hugh and his wife sitting out in the pavement cafe which belonged to the hotel, nearly empty at this hour.

"Join us for a last coffee?"

The man waved his plump, pink hand. His face was, despite its width, handsome, if a little florid; the light blue eyes curiously moist. His wife, elegant with a side sweep of dark brown hair, wore a long, cool silk frock and leather Moroccan sandals.

Judith stopped, put down her small overnight bag.

"Thanks. I think we will."

"Good. Enjoy the mountains?"

"Oh yes. Yes, we did. It was most interesting."

"We know the mountain villages well. We love it up there – usually take a trip. We have Moroccan friends we stay with."

"Really?" Judith was surprised. She did not associate this urbane, silk-suited couple with the kinds of hillside, red-mud hovels she had seen and which privately she had found shocking. There had been a quality of dank despair in some of those places that was not attractive; even, she and her daughter had been threatened with a knife in a squalid back alley, for money, of course, but she had resisted the threats and let out a volley of heated Russian – a language she knew well – to confuse the man. Beatrice

43

was impressed by her mother, and had been a little more conciliatory ever since.

"Yes." Hugh's wife held out her slim, pretty feet. "Look."

In the darkness of the terrace, Judith could not quite make out what she was being shown. Remembering, she flicked the yellow lighter and peered. She could see a faint tracery of lines, a pattern like a sort of reddish-brown netting all over Dorothy's feet.

"I had it done in the village when we were there last week," said the woman. "My friend's sister does it. Moroccan women have their hands decorated too – it's a sign of great beauty."

"Oh." Judith was confounded. It seemed rather absurd to try to enter a culture of which so clearly one was not in the least a part. In this instant, her respect for the couple diminished a degree.

The conversation turned to the all-embracing poverty, the beggars; they compared the dreadful sights they had seen, outdoing in each other's stories of third world horror.

"The boy – Samir," said Judith. "Do you know him well?"

The man hesitated. The wet, pale eyes flicked to his wife and back to Judith.

"No," he said at last. "This is the first time we've seen him here. I don't know much about him. We – do what we can."

"I think you're incredibly kind to him. Nobody else would take so much trouble."

Hugh flapped a wide hand, looked down at his knees; the soft puckered lids with their camel lashes half closed over the light eyes.

"Nonsense! It isn't much – and I'm sure you'd do as much if we weren't here."

"Yes, perhaps I would" Judith leaned forward, earnest, leaning deeper into the theme. "Do you know, I passed a beggar woman the other day and I thought she was about seventy. She was so shrivelled and scrawny and bent. When she lifted aside her head-cloth, I saw she was suckling a child! She had two other young children with her. Probably they'd been sitting on that pavement for hours – near that swanky Casino. Well, I just emptied my pockets – gave her all the spare change I had."

Hugh's heavy face flushed and the boyish eyes brimmed with emotion. He turned to his wife, clasped her hands, looked at Judith's daughter and dabbed at the tears.

"You have a lovely mother, young lady," he said. "A beautiful, wonderful mother."

Judith's daughter wriggled own into the wicker chair in embarrassment. Despite the bravado up in the mountains, her mother didn't strike her as wonderful, or lovely, or any such thing – just mildly dotty and getting worse. Earlier that day she had nearly lost her expensive watch in yet another encounter with a young girl, begging with her blind grandfather in tow.

"Darling, you can easily buy another," her mother had said, as the girl pointed to the branded western timepiece.

"That's not the point." Beatrice had stamped her foot, making the blind old man shrink back in alarm. "I like this watch, we need it on holiday. And anyway – it gives them ideas."

"Ideas!" Judith had sighed in vexation, scorn. "Oh, very well. Keep your blessed watch."

And another little schism ran between them, another faint hairline fissure that appeared stealthily along the seam of their mutual, unspoken disunity.

Now, Dorothy yawned and stretched her hennaed feet.

"Time for bed, sweet," she said to her husband.

The slender, smooth hand rested for a moment on his shoulder. Was it possible, Judith thought, was she just very slightly digging in those long nails; was there just a faint, pointed pressure there? "Sidi Abdullah will be locking the grilles soon."

Edward sighed.

"Everything closes so damned early in Morocco," he said. "That's the only thing I don't like about the place. Ten thirty at night and the street are as dead as a door-nail."

"Just as well, my love," replied his wife, bland, saccharine.

The painted nails retreated and the couple made their goodnights, leaving Judith to the quiet, dim cafe front for a few moments. What was going on there? A drink problem, perhaps? Gambling? You could satisfy both those cravings at the Casino, even at this hour, and until the early hours of the morning, and you could, she was sure, pay the concierge or the duty manager to open up for you at any time. Perhaps this was what those sharp fingernails were clawing him away from?

Judith's daughter also yawned, loudly and without grace. She heaved her long-boned, big-footed body out of the wicker, which gave up its thanks at deliverance in a plethora of small twitches and creaks, and slung her cotton jacket over her shoulder.

"Bed, mother! Or you'll be too tired to want to know in the morning."

"Right, dear. Yes. All right."

Judith was irritated, as usual; but as usual she obeyed. The hovering night porter pulled the grilles to, shut them with a clang, and the hotel lights dimmed. No drunken home comers or unseemly brawls disturbed the warm, misty tranquillity of the square.

* * *

The following day was mercifully cooler. Judith abandoned the sulking Beatrice and determined on a tour of exploration before the weather should heat up again. She breakfasted rather late, and the dining room was already empty. Sidi, ever courteous, informed her that Blanche had stayed in their room, having started with "A very fierce head pain. *Migraine,*" he finished, in French.

"And her husband?"

"Ah, Mr. Edward, he goes out – somewhere. In the city, perhaps."

Judith contemplated this. She did not, for whatever reason, want to come across Edward today; she would enjoy herself more if she was not forced to make conversation, but first, she thought, she must find a guide; it was not a good idea to wander the intricate maze of the old town without one.

The guide – supplied by the Tourist Office – was voluble, had but one rather rickety tooth, was markedly in a state of senility and, finally, was particularly boring. He took Judith on a horse and trap ride round the old sights, stopping for minutes at a time to describe in thick, patois French some dull and to her unremarkable gateway, Bab this, Bab that; and failing utterly to comprehend Judith's desire to stop and explore, to take photographs of some piles of pots and pans in an obscure corner of the medina.

At length, she made him wait in a street, out of which many of the smaller alleys led.

"I wish to walk a little," she said.

"It is dangerous," said the guide, sullenly, feeling his mastery of the situation ebbing from him. He opened his mouth wide, and hooked a skinny finger behind the one, blackening tooth, and proceeded to pick at it as if dismissing Judith from his affairs.

"I shan't go far, promised Judith, "and you must wait for me. Don't drive off, please."

"As if I would leave you!" The guide was genuinely shocked, wagging the lean, stubbly jaw up and down in vigorous protest.

Judith smiled, and set off to investigate. Soon she realised what they meant, all those warnings. This was worse than a maze, it became more like an underground warren, dark, foetid, with appalling smells that rose up suddenly from the gutters and hit the stomach. It wasn't very thrilling, and she was being stared at by the inhabitants, who looked at her with passive hostility.

She must get out; it was, she admitted, a mistake to have come, and the airlessness of these stuffy quarters was beginning to make her feel choked. There was a patch of brighter light, beyond the end of the alley she was in – it surely represented more or less where she had entered this darkened tumble of lanes. Landmarks were difficult to identify, but Judith somehow groped her way back up. A particularly foul stench made her gasp; the mid-day heat was inducing vertigo. She stopped, leaned on a wall, covering her nose and mouth with her light scarf, closed her eyes for a moment against the darkness, the stink, against everything that was where she stood.

When she opened her eyes again, she saw that she was directly opposite a kind of lowish tunnel that led between two buildings. It was darker than the alley and for a moment Judith could make out nothing at all. Then, inevitably, as the eyes adjusted, shapes made themselves clear, becoming clearer, and it was then that she saw them. At first, only him, with his unmistakable bulk, his light suit and that feathery fringe of hair; and after, in painful imprint, a kneeling Samir, smaller, darker, more vibrant in the dimness..

She heard, rather than distinctly saw what was happening, and yet later the picture in her mind was a sharp as if she had had a spotlight. Every detail on the frame was there, for always, as if it had been taken under the harshest noon sun that burned beyond the passageways. She would never forget. Confused, hot and ashamed – though of what, she did not know – Judith scuttled up the narrow lanes, her scarf pressed tight to her face, rejoined her cabby guide. He looked at her sickly countenance and sneered maliciously.

"I knew you would not enjoy it," he said, and cracked his whip.

Back at the hotel, Judith went to their room, lay on the hard bed and tried to keep herself still, to unwind that dreadful sickening knot in her belly. She supposed there was money in it for Samir; though you couldn't tell.

After the early evening prayer call, she took her daughter out for a meal somewhere else; she did not want to see the English couple. Anyway, it was time to leave this place.

* * *

When they breakfasted in the morning, they learned that Edward and Blanche had departed.

"To visit friends elsewhere, maybe Agadir," said Sidi. "They know a lot of people here."

"I can imagine they do," said Judith. She wondered how often Dorothy had to move him on.

"Will you order us a horse-cab to the station?" she asked.

Sidi bowed, smiled, and they bought gifts from the hotel shop When the cab drew up, there was Samir, white teeth, brilliant eyes, bare dusty feet. For all the world, an untainted angel.

"Goodbye, Madame." Samir managed this in English, and ran to open the cab door.

"Oh – Samir." Judith paused, conflicted.

"Madame?" The sunny face suddenly anxious.

"Here are some dirum for you."

And her reward was the radiant beam, the curious little bow. Yes, irresistible. Despite herself, Judith wanted to touch him. She hugged the boy briefly, looking into his clear, untroubled eyes.

Oh, Samir.

On the train, disturbing images crowded at her vision; it was difficult to concentrate on her reading. To quell the faint nausea that curdled in her stomach she reached into her pocket for a mint. Encountered something harder, larger than a sweet. It was the disposable lighter – the offering from Samir. Her fingers clenched it, gripped the small, cheap talisman; felt her jaw contract and the sickness rise.

Abruptly, Judith stood up, rived her way out of the compartment, past polite travellers, leaned in the corridor near the doorway and watched the passing landscape as they rolled smoothly beyond the city, out into the yellow sand moonscape of the edges of the Sahara. Soon they reached a station, a large mainline connection with many, criss-crossing routes. The doors opened and the usual crush of passengers hurled themselves off and onto the train. Wrenching open the far side door, Judith grasped the lighter tightly and hurled it strongly away from her, out of the train and into a wide parabola. The thing curved high, flashed briefly in the bright sun, then dived out of sight to clatter faintly on the far side of the tracks.

Doors were closed; the train slid on. Judith returned to her daughter in the packed carriage. Beatrice had met an American on that last day, a large, rather pleasant young man who was going to meet her at their next destination. She was cheerful, chatty, animated, the elongated heavy bones assuming a sudden surprising athletic grace.

Judith resettled herself with her book. Her daughter chattered on.

"I just loved Marrakech, didn't you, Ma? I really liked it there. We must come again – Denby says he's probably going in the Autumn. I say, we really have to come again. What do you think, Ma?"

Judith looked up, glanced out of the window at the passing dunes with their clean, sharp lines against the unclouded sky and the sporadic groves of palms. It was a strange landscape, one she did not understand.

"Perhaps," she said, and returned to her book.

BLONDE BOMBSHELL

HER HAIR WAS blonde.

Well, some of it was blonde.

If one is to be held to the strictest veracity, some of it was blondeish; and what was not was promptly, meticulously, assiduously helped to become so; that which, again abiding by the most stringent truth, was dulling and fading albeit ever so slightly was encouraged to more positively platinum by he application of fluids from little bottles and sometimes, though rarely, visits to the hairdresser. She preferred to affect these changes herself, so that one could with clear conscience maintain that this was only the most modest of adaptations, really nothing very much, so simple that one could do it in half an hour in one's own bathroom. A mere realignment of nature's true intention.

She was thirty-one. Well, almost.

In four months' time   to be pedantic, four months and twenty-one days – she would have her birthday. The thought struck her with reverberating waves of panic, like the shock echoes of a medium-scale earthquake. Her entry into the fourth decade of her life had been passed, coped with, the mighty tremors of that particular anniversary assimilated into a new vibrancy of living, new vigour which might even, if one looked very closely, suggest a determination so strong as to suggest something akin to violence in those energetic exploits. But now there was the nasty feeling that each year hence would produce this returning quiver, this unhappy reminder that no longer could one say with airy confidence, "I'm just turned thirty, as a matter of fact."

So Araminta (her mother had been addicted to the romantic novel, and had gone so far as to design herself a ravishing death-bed outfit of peach satin and pearls, which alas will never be realised as the unfortunate lady, though of course she does not presently know it, will drown at sea) – so Araminta contemplates herself at nearly, not quite, soon to be thirty-one.

Full length, in the mirror.

Outside her shuttered apartment windows, downstairs in the hot bleached street, are the voices of children, woken from their summer siesta to come, drowsy still and sticky, to run off sleep and sweat in the coooling air of the later afternnoon, that will slip quite suddenly into the long warm night.

"San-dra!"

The harsh, high, child's Spanish makes Araminta smile. Sandra, so frequently hailed, she has never knowingly seen; but the habitual plaintive cry floats up past the geraniumed balconies and bears for Araminta its own, particular memories of this time.

"Sandrrra, venga!""

A brief, rare silence in the cacophony below.

Then, other voices.

"Vas a la piscina?"

"Si, si. Claro."

"OK. Vamos!"

"Yo tambien! Sandra, esperame!"

"No quiero nadar contigo! No te quiero."

"Ah, Sandra!"

Ah, Sandra, indeed, thinks Araminta, with a wry almost-thirty-one-years-old grimace. One wants, the other doesn't. It starts in childhood, and then you're stuck with it.

Araminta – often nicknamed Harry by her friends at

school, but this she is working hard to forget – turns again to the reflection in the peeling mirror. Swivels to view this side, that. Full frontal. From the rear – twisting her blonded head to study the sturdy buttocks, firm muscular thighs. Flicks up her head, adjudges the neck and chin.

Not bad. Good, in fact. Very good. Silkily, smoothly brown, she is a golden girl. The sun does much at this time of the year, good old Zeus, that the little bottles must take over in the paler days of winter. Armainta might even, if one were to take the rather old-fashioned, vulgar slang of the years of her infancy, those days when her romantically afflicted mother sighed over the squarely-built child, might even have been called a true "Blonde Bombshell". Certainly there was enough packed in there to make one think of explosions.

"Well done, Araminta Winter," she says, and gives herself the brisk approbation that her games teacher used to do.

"Well done, Araminta. We'll put you forward for the Junior Olympic Diving team this year."

"Hurrah for Araminta Winter! Glory for the school!"

Medals, applause, cheers and glory for Araminta.

All that sport has done her proud; she is well-shaped, if perhaps a little sturdy for some tastes, she has excellent muscle tone, and she is healthy, shining healthy, a welcome quality in contrast to the skin and bone, seemingly anorexic, pallid catwalk girls. Moreover, since her college days, Araminta has managed to slough off some of that possible over-athletic image and to clad herself instead in a sort of extravagant femaleness; not the pastel, soft-focus heroine of her mother's dreams, but an altogether more robust style that leaves men gaping and, in some place, following her hopefully down the street. Those strong, highly-toned calves, those proudly arched feet step out

like a fiesta horse in the white and gold stilettos; that perfect waist and the firm, protruding rump in the classic
tight skirts that Araminta wears along with flamboyantly
colourful tops; that well-developed, swimmer's bosom -

Wait a moment.

Araminta frowns, puckers her pert Puck face. Something is wrong.

Turn to the side. Now the other. Again.

Araminta steps closer to the mirror, her full pouting
mouth open like a child's, her eyes, blue as the summer
sea and blue enough to satisfy the most critical of romantic
writers, agog. Closer she peers, as if by breathing on her
mirrored image she can dispel what she thinks she saw,
what she is horribly sure she saw just then.

Surely not? Surely it cannot be, after all that aquatic exercise, all those championship marathons? But yes. The
cornflower eyes (a sure-fire Cartland epithet of some comfort to her mother) squint most unromantically at the evi-
dence she does not want to see.

Oh Araminta Winter! Your breasts are beginning to sag.

Not a very great deal, only a tad; but the things are
heavy with pectoral muscle (the breast-stroke her competition best) and there is, side-on, a faintly noticeable droop.

Thoughtful Araminta picks up her brassiere, winches it
up a couple of notches as a good sailor tacks in a sloppy,
slackened sail, and gets dressed to go out.

* * *

Two months later, Araminta has a beau.

That is, to put it in terms less reminiscent of one of her
mother's favourite novels (a framework in which it must
be confessed she sometimes likes to see herself) she is into
a full-blooded sexual liaison, engaged in with all the pow-

56

erful energy of which her strong, working body is capable. This is considerable, and leaves many lesser men beached and gasping, not in desire for more of Araminta but for an ordinary, mortal woman.

Araminta's beau is American and quite appallingly rich, some years older than Araminta and very, very good-looking. Let's say, he has light brown hair carelessly and naturally streaked with a darker and more mellow blonde than Araminta's bottles can produce, bright light brown eyes and a wide, quick smile that sits nicely on the American rugged jaw. Generally, he is the sort of man that women put straight into their phones and their address books, and for whom they purchase a landline telephone answering service so that they do not miss his call.

His name is Harrison Clive, which confuses everyone in England where they do not like such verbal trickery, and he and Araminta have laughed early on, in their first real conversation following the meeting at Jessica's drinks party, which was itself followed by an immediate, lusty and hugely mutually satisfactory encounter between the sheets.

"Say, you're a Harry too? But then, we don't use that shortening in the States – they only call me that in England."

"In that case I shall call you Harrison," said Araminta, only just stopping herself in time from adding "always". "And for the record, I too prefer my proper name. In full."

"Fine, sure." Harrison having dealt with this minor point offloaded it from the computer bank of his mind in the way that Americans in business so easily do. (Americans, if they are going to be neurotic, do so on a grand scale. Either something is worth going over the top about, and then you would get yourself Woody Allen's analyst, or it should not be afforded more than five seconds' attention. In this way, they do not go in for the long-drawn-out tedious inconclusive fretting of the English.)

After this, they fell to screwing again, and another couple of months passed.

It turned out that Harrison was quite disgustingly, abhorrently wealthy, with various apartments and houses (mansions) scattered around the globe so that he could follow the gently warmer weather and maintain that even, smooth, honeyed tan: so different from the amateur sunseeker's mahogany among the merely nouvea-medium-riche who do not know what to do with it all except build a Costa villa and expose themselves at all times to the very harshest sun in the glaring mid-day Spanish summer.

He had a boat, too. Of course. It was a very large boat, bordering on being a ship, Araminta thought, with resident crew who obligingly sailed this floating idyll to wherever he happened to be, or to wanted to be, in the world. He bought Araminta the merest trifle, a trinket of white gold, diamonds and sapphires when she was out buying fresh leeks and lamb for dinner one day, and in terms of their relative incomes, the transactions were roughly equivalent.

Very soon, Araminta had moved into Harrison's ranch house in the quieter hills, away from the brash, tiresome Costa, and within an amazingly short time she had become accustomed to all this, even to having her shoes cleaned by the Filipino house servants. She also visited his homes in the West Indies, California and New York, as well as sprawling beach bungalows capriciously bought and sometimes re-sold in other, more obscure locations. They did not visit the London apartment much, and hardly ever the Scottish island (complete with refurbished castle) he had also bought on whim as the weather was rarely good enough, though Hogmanay was a tradition Harrison liked to indulge in: "my Scottish roots".

"Are you happy, honey?" he asked her from time to time.

"Not a bit. Entirely miserable."

Then they laughed and laughed, and hit and bit each other, and screwed some more.

* * *

There is only one snag to all this bliss. After all, the ingredients are there as to a publishing-house formula. Attractive, young-ish blonde (ish) English girl goes to work on the Costa, meets older, rich American. They fall in love. The sun shines three hundred and fifty eight and a half days a year. What more is there to write? (The bodice-ripper, of course, spins this out for a couple of hundred pages, with some early problems of mutual antagonism and misunderstandings; but the end result would read the same.)

So what in the world can be the matter with Araminta Winter? Why has she begun to worry, inwardly, secretly nursing her festering anxiety so that the almost imperceptible crease lines have deepened round her cornflower eyes (in which men would willingly drown) and even along the sides of her sensual mouth, across her religiously moisturised forehead; all of these acquiring a dangerous hint of permanence?

Why does she laugh a little too loudly again, effervesce rather too fizzily, dive into the deep jade pool a bit too heartily? And why, oh why, does she toss and turn in the vast bed, crumpling the peach satin sheets and clutching the luxury feather pillows in her long varnished nails, until Harrison is provoked to remark mildly that if he'd wanted a whale for a bedmate he sure could have gotten one easily enough.

It is the view in the mirror that haunts her, that day in her former apartment, in her former life, on that sultry afternoon at the end of a summer or so ago, when Araminta listened to twelve-year-old Sandra spurn thirteen-year-old Marcos, and when almost in the next second, so that the events were linked irrevocably and evocatively in her mind, she recognised her own body's duplicity. So fragile is life, so tenuous one's contentment, balanced like a spinning twopence; we should hold our breaths when life is good, when we catch ourselves merry – the coin will fall at any moment flat to the table.

That view in the mirror, and that alone, has been sufficient to set off Araminta's lone imaginings, that solitary, night-time terror. She is getting old! Already, at now well past thirty-one, her body is betraying her. Further inspections have been furtively carried out and alas, have confirmed this unpleasant suspicion. She is sure almost certain, that the breasts have sagged a little more, another millimetre south. What is to be done?

Now surely, the bagging of a multi-millionaire for her lover (soon to be her husband, we'll get married the moment the lawyers sort out the divorce settlement, honey) should have reassured her, one would think. All that dosh should buffet her against the insecurities of the regular mortal, or what else is being super wealthy all about?

But Harrison likes perfection. How long before he notices that his Araminta, his golden bird, is not quite a perfect specimen, not the escort he is worthy of hanging on his arm? And he can, naturally, afford perfection.

At this thought, the gloom around Arminta lifts. That's it. Of course.

"Harrison."

"Honey?"

They lie amongst the black satin sheets (Harrison's

choice for tonight) after what has been a most unusual session. Harrison is therefore at his most relaxed; innovation whether in business or pleasure, is always gratifying to his restless ego state.

"Harrison, I want to ask you something."

"Thought there's something on your mind. You've been – weird for a few weeks."

"Well," said Araminta, tracking his smooth, immaculately browned back with a fingernail. Oh, the injustice of things! Why don't men age in the same way? "Well, let me ask you a question first. Have you noticed anything different about me? Anything that might have changed."

There is a silence whilst Harrison gives this enquiry the fifteen seconds he gauges it would have been worth at a board meeting, twelve of these being out of courtesy for the speaker, and replies that he has not.

"Nope. Not a thing."

"Are you sure?"

And Araminta springs from the bed, stands before him, slowly pirouetting so that from his prone position he will have an unspoilt, decisive view of the trouble zone.

"Absolutely. You look just A-One to me."

Strong tanned arms grab for her, but Araminta is having none of that. She skips inches away.

"Harrison. My tits are beginning to sag."

"The heck they are. C'mere."

"No, Harrison. They're definitely drooping . I'm going to get old, and they'll be round my waist, and all that muscle will turn to horrible fat and drag them down, and you won't want to be seen with me at the pool, it wouldn't matter so much if we lived in England, that's the ironic part, and my skin will be wrinkled and repulsive and you won't love me any more."

Araminta does not even have to affect the tears she had

planned at this pathetic point of the story; they are utterly and quite real, as are her fears. This is her romantic dream that she is living, and she does not want to find herself in a geriatric nightmare instead.

"That's absurd. Araminta, you're being ridiciouls. You know I love you for yourself. It's not just the way you look – though I might add I see nothing wrong, nothing wrong at all in a man liking a cute, five-foot seven-inch blue-eyed blonde with an arse on her like – "

"Harrison, you're disgusting."

"I know it. Get back in bed and be disgusting with me."

And that, for the moment, is the end of that.

* * *

But of course, Araminta continued to fret in the way that so many women do; driven by their biology to remember their bodies' inner timetables and upheavals, they are thus more involved with the body's outer shell, they feel it from within and worry more about their physicality. This is, of course, why the image-makers are so successful. Add to this a curious notion, of an origin hard to determine, that roughly half the world's population – that is the female half – must conform to roughly the same shape, dimensions and general appearance, and you have a recipe for the hysteria into which poor Araminter Winter was fast sinking.

"Honey."

Harrison was a patient man; he could afford to be, and indeed had built his fortune in part on just this quality; but his tolerance had limits, and in any case, women's things bored him.

"Hun, I told you before. I love you for yourself, for your gorgeous, beautiful self, and I don't give a shit whether your boobs hang around your knees. It's you I'm going to marry, in a couple of months or so, when the settlement's through. Not a cardboard cut-out of Miss Ideal Costa. It's Miss Araminta Winter, warts and all, that I'm going for."

This beautiful speech, though outwardly reassuring, was not strictly truthful. Araminta suspected as much, her deep, mysterious biological forces on the alert and telling her that Harrison Clive would not be seen dead with a woman whose breasts lolloped to her nether regions. Harrison suspected that Araminta suspected his speciousness, and so they kissed each other particularly passionately and screwed hastily, avidly, to seal over the jagged edges of the moment.

Two more mirror inspections proved fatal for the finely strung tension of Aramainta's self esteem. In the middle of a rather cold December night she sat up in her sleep, opened her wide large mouth and yelled.

"I want them fixed, Harrison. I want them done."

* * *

Harrison was not a mean man; he had no need to be (though often multi-millionaires are extremely stingy) and the few thousand it cost in a private clinic was less than a dewdrop in the financially upward mobility of his affairs.

So it was that Araminta succumbed eagerly, even as one going to a holy sacrifice, to the surgeon's knife. It was done in London, quietly, discreetly. When she returned, her outward appearance was the same. A little more thrusting, perhaps, more aggression up top, as it were; but it could just have been a better brassiere.

It was on the beach, by the pool, in scanty summer wear that the value of those paltry few thousands really showcased the investment. Jutting like twin prows of some sturdy ship, those silicone miracles were as firm and as hard as well-slung coconuts, with the protuberant brown nipples, forced ever forwards, perched cheekily on the ends.

"God, will you look at that uplift?"

Other women on the beach muttered, watching the bounding Araminta through slitted, sun-blinded eyes.

"Unnatural, I'd say. Look at the way that bikini top stays on, and without straps.

But the most startling effect of all was when Araminta lay flat on her back to sunbathe. Breasts, as a rule, sprawl sideways on these occasions, flatten, disappear into the general mass of spreadeagled torso like sloppy fried eggs; but Araminta's new, improved structure stood out firmly in the form of two pointed lumps of an unreal consistency and announced themselves to the bright overhead sky.

"They stick up like sandcastles," they muttered unkindly, in the way that people do. The female part of the beach population, that is. The men simply stared and felt that inexplicable warm, moist itching of the palms that troubles them in such moments.

Araminta Winter was justifiably, overwhelmingly proud of the success of the project, and showed it off at all possible opportunities. Beach dresses became mere skimpy pieces of gauze, tied provocatively above the thrusting pyramids. Topless sunning was not a problem. Her insecurities were, needless to say, quite gone. The sky was forever cloudless again, life was consummate.

* * *

Though of course, it wasn't.

A year, two years, three years later, and little cracks were beginning to appear. Oh, not in Araminta's wonderful bosom (whose two thin moon-shaped underscars didn't show a bit, thanks to having invested in the best surgeon for the job). But in other ways, her utopia was showing signs of strain. Perfection is a very tall order.

"You know," said Harrison Clive one morning over breakfast, "I think we should change the colour scheme of the jet. I'm pretty sick of looking at those mustard seats. I'm thinking a classier colour."

"But we only had them done a year ago."

Araminta protested with the lingering traces of a frugal, lower-middle-class background where leftover custard was preserved, to be eaten cold on tomorrow's jelly.

"Well, I've decided." Harrison slapped a passing fly with his white napkin. "And whilst we're talking improvements, I think we should do something with your hair. If you'll pardon me saying it."

"My *hair?*" Araminta blinked. The fly dropped like a bomb to the marble terrace, where it struggled in its final, limb-wriggling contortions. "But you've always liked it blonde. They way it is naturally," she added. The fly twitched once, lay still, stiffening by the instant.

"Bit passe," said Harrison. "Doesn't go with our new image. Looked at some fashion glossies the other day. Nineties Euro-trash out. Something more subtle in. I'll book you at Rafael's from the office."

"The office" – some sort of import-export business Araminta only vaguely understood – was Harrison's new venture. Started as an idle hobby, to keep him from the boredom of only making money all the time, and to siphon off some of that taxable income, it already looked set to make a whole new fortune by itself, and it kept him pretty busy. Araminta did not see as much of him these days, though she always accompanied him on promotional trips. It was very upmarket – "exporting for the discerning entrepreneur" – something that appealed to the already super-rich, also eager to channel their money away from predatory tax revenue personnel in their own countries.

Perfection. Discretion. Of product and image.

Thus Araminta found her hair clucked over, tutted over, fussed over, tweaked and rebuked.

"Such dry ends! How *could* we have let it?"

Mercilessly the chiding, punishing fingers cut, snipped, scissored, sawed great hunks of hair into a plain, simple shape, the colour toned down ("and don't you dare go at it yourself again or Vivian will be *very* cross!") to a sort of tawny-gold shade which suited her, it was true, but it had to be said that the whole effect was to shift her into another age bracket. Less of the cute-assed blonde, more of the elegant wife.

But Harrison approved; that was all that mattered.

Next it was the clothes. A whole new wardrobe (or what would have been four or five to the average woman) appeared, to suit the new look. The startling breasts were more concealed, though their fine shape and prominence still showed under silk, cashmere and fine leather. Out went the flimsy beachwear under Harrison's disdainful hand ("We don't want to look like a bimbo, honey") and in came classy one-pieces, high cut on the leg, with complementing beach jackets. Araminta wept for her beach-blonde freedom, but Harrison was unmoving, unmoved. Those magnificent knockers were for Harrison's pleasure alone. Araminta could not but think this was a terrible waste of money, akin to keeping the leftover custard permanently in the fridge.

The revamped, regroomed Araminta, the honeyed hair shining and swinging, her shapely legs covered in fine dusky stockings and those high stepping feet tamed into costly medium-heeled gunmetal pumps, slipped into a cashmere suit and a silk blouse, hung herself with pearls, real, old pearls ("get rid of that flashy diamond junk") and presented herself to Harrison for a business lunch.

"Perfect," murmured Harrison Clive, fingering his silvering side streaks of soft hair. "You look absolutely perfect, my dear."

The kiss bestowed felt strangely reverent, as one might kiss one's mother, or older sister, or a distant aunt. Through Araminta's still quick bright mind there flashed the rebel thought: perfect for what? And immediately that artful mind censored it. Do not argue. You have what you have.

The nights amid the black, peach, cream or apple-green sheets were still good, though. Here all could be abandoned, all that daytime effort, all notions of image forgotten in the naked, leaping sexuality. Here they could be as crude, as lewd, as rude as ever they wanted, and Araminta was happy.

* * *

Two, three years on; and Araminta is at that age which women dread – men too, though few would admit to it. When one cannot pretend to be "just turned", "almost, nearly". She is on the long, slow run-up to middle age.

The wondrous breasts have lived up to all the surgeon's promises, and still protrude cheerily, startlingly, from Araminta's thorax. Not a sign of wear, despite frequent and rough handling by the energetic, seemingly ageless Harrison Clive. He of course, is getting better by the year, the deepening lines by the generous, firm mouth merely reminding women irresistibly of Robert Redford and all those men whom Nature seems to favour in her most splendid autumn.

And Araminta's little doubts creep up on her again, at first very slightly, such as could easily be brushed aside;

and then more persistently drumming at her in the night until they are a crowd, thronging into her sleep so that once again she wallows and wrestles in the wide bed until Harrison is driven into one of the spare rooms.

"Just what is the matter with you?" says Harrison after one such particularly trying night. "For Godssake, woman, you've all you could ever want. Just what in Heaven's name are you anxious about now?"

This time, he is prepared to allot her quite a good slice of executive time. At least five minutes. By now, he is genuinely fond of Araminta. She still looks good, she does just as he requires of a female escort of a suitable age (he is not, as he stated, into bimbos and is after all considerably more mature himself these days) and she is far and away the best in bed he's ever had, being intelligent as well as robustly sensual. He is, in short, absolutely content with her, has frequently told her so. What in Hell's teeth can she be looking for?

But Harrison cares. He genuinely cares that Araminta is troubled and when she sobs and snuffles into a corner of the white satin sheets – a bridal night – Harrison patiently fetches the Kleenex, dries her nose carefully first, and offers her his manly shoulder.

"H-H-H-Harrison," cried Araminta in great stricken gasps. "It's my bottom!"

"Your *what*, for Christssake?"

"My bottom. It's sagging, dropping, going South. Look!"

And as in all those years before, Araminta stands bronzed, naked and lovely before him. Slowly, she rotates, and this time, it cannot be denied. Against the firm, uplifted outward shove of the bosom, Araminta's rear looks sadly out of line. Where the breasts push upward, the buttocks seem determined to sink in the opposite direction, giving the hitherto sexy hindquarters a slightly square, defeated appearance. Unpleasant creases are also evident on the tops of her thighs where the haunches rest.

"Yup," says Harrison, making one of the masterful, swift executive decisions for which he is so well known. "See what you mean. And don't worry – "

as Araminta's large mouth opens,

" – we'll get them fixed."

* * *

Life went on serenely for another few years. The buttocks stood proud and firm with passing of time, pushing backwards and slightly up to counterbalance the marvellous frontispiece. Once more, Araminta looked a whole. She turned the dreaded age of forty with ease, secure in the love of Harrison and the skilled hands of her surgeon; or it could have been the other way around. "Specialist in beauty maintenance," the good doctor's card announced. "I simply help you ladies maintain what you already have. Nothing more. Yours is the beauty – I merely serve it." What could be more loving than that?

By now the various houses and apartments, the jet, the boat and the Scottish island had all be furbished and re-furbished, along with Araminta's seasonally changing wardrobe – flat pumps this year, long swirling skirts in expensive fabrics, throw that vulgar tight power-dressing stuff out – and still Harrison Clive managed to sustain an effortless perfection.

It was, thought Araminta one peri-menopausal day, very wearing. She had reached that time where ladies tend to feel tired and somehow easily dispirited, libido plunging suddenly into an abyss of hormonal emptiness. Orgasms were harder to achieve, less sought after; uncharacteristically, Armainta was happy to lie back and half enjoy it, her thoughts tending to drift onto altogether different things. Harrison noticed this, naturally, and all by himself. Araminta did not need to thresh about in the night or weep. His sexual needs were for more than a passive lump of designer flesh that lay under him floating off to sleep.

So they went to the best Hormone Replacement specialist, who righted the balance skilfully (and expensively) and soon put fire back into the right parts. They took the opportunity to have her neck and chin done ("Just the mererest *hint* of a *tiny* nip and tuck of the lower face is all Mrs. Clive needs to retain her marvellous bone structure") which cheered her up as much as the little pills they gave her. Everybody said how radiant she was looking.

"Mind you, she can afford to"

"Huh! What could you or I look like with him behind us?"

"Well, I daresay. But she's a very pretty woman anyway. For her age."

"Maybe. But have you seen his new PA? Now there's something! And not an operation scar in sight."

Ho-hum, people will be bitchy. None of it bothered Araminta; she had reached that plateau of tolerance where she could recognise such statements for what they were. The truth. And, like injections, the truth doesn't hurt if you don't flinch from it. Indeed, you hardly notice it, so fleeting is the pinprick. No, but something else was bothering Araminta Clive (as she had, latterly, finally become). Restless nights began again; hormone therapy was stepped up; she flew to England, to America, for some weeks in the best health farms. Yet still her sleep, with or without Harrison, was troubled.

* * *

70

One afternoon, Araminta Winter-Clive happens to be sitting in the garden of an old school friend in England. It is a large, untidy garden somewhere in Sussex and the summer is unusually hot. Araminta has just emerged from the latest health spa, which included a group therapy activity for women of her age and condition It has irritated her profoundly.

The friend's house is also untidy, the kitchen in particular big, disorganised and full of things being used, just having been used, about to be used or, regrettably, having been used rather a log time ago and not consigned to the washing up. Parts of it are frankly dirty. Filthy, if one were to be brutally honest. Araminta looks round in critical disdain. Harrison would have ten thousand fits, and he would employ an army of gardeners immediately to landscape the exterior into well-ordered obedience and scenic regularity.

It so happens that the friend is also untidy and in some parts dirty. The strong, greying hair is pushed back into a hurried knot, the chin that sags plumply into a corrugated neck; her bosom hangs heavy, to her waist, her bottom broad and her midriff expanded to the full width of her considerable hips. Grimed with house-dust and coal from the huge double Aga which dominates the kitchen, Rachel's reddened hands fold placidly on her aproned lap, and her kaftan cotton dress slides aimlessly round her slackening body. She looks her age, she looks fifteen years older than Araminta, she looks a sight.

Araminta has a sudden vision of herself without the care and control of the dedicated surgeon, the attention of the clever hormone specialist, looking rather similar; she reflects upon Harrison Clive and his probable reactions, and shudders.

And then, there are the grandchildren. There is a deluge of them, a tsunami of grubby tots in rompers, torn and patched dungarees with buttons missing or little pants, or sometimes, unfortunately and unhygienically, no pants at all; in the midst of the chaos, a rampantly excitable dog. Various sticky messes everywhere. It is not exactly perfection.

Thank goodness, says Araminta inwardly, for my life, and for Harrison Clive.

But even then she does not sleep, even in the huge, squashy, admittedly comfortable bed in her friend's house where in the hastily-cleared guest bedroom she lies staring at the dim shapes of boxes, soft toys, and heaps of clothing between her and the window, where outside the dark summer trees swish to and fro in the now quiet garden and small creatures scuttle about.

Thus Araminta does a lot of thinking in those long night hours when the bright Sussex moon slides placidly across the breathless August sky. Pale-eyed, she rises for breakfast – chaos, warm muffins, treacled infants everywhere and armfuls of fresh roses and lavender brought in from the garden by daughters in country maid smocks, one at least barely disguising another embryonic grandchild – and drinks sweet tea with her friend who, sensing that Araminta is upset, says little but also thinks a great deal.

* * *

Unaccustomedly, dangerously relaxed, Araminta returned to the Spanish villa. Oh beware of relaxing, Araminta! Harrison and his like never relax; that way you might get to know who you really are.

The palm-flagged drive greeted her as usual with its friendly waving fronds, its gravel neatly raked, each smooth pebble meekly arraigned in its appointed place.

The marble floors shone and the walls dazzled whitely in their silence, whilst a heavy scent of bougainvillea swam up to her quivering nose.

Harrison Clive appeared on the steps. His skin, more golden smooth than before, etched the Redford lines with heartbreaking definition, hair newly shaped in some immaculate, youthful style. The cream, lightweight trousers and fine cambric shirt sat perfect and uncreased upon his perfect body.

The perfect evening appetising drink was put into Araminta's insensible hand.

"You look marvellous, hon." Harrison delivered the respectful Continental double kiss, the housekeeper being present and the chauffeur still within earshot. "That health place in England sure knows its stuff. And that skirt thing – well it's just *perfect.*"

At which, Araminta turned, swivelled upon one exquisite brocade pump. Whirled round full circle, sending waves of cool air from the fan of her wide crepe georgette skirt (Harrods). Screamed. Threw the glass and its slightly sickly aromatic contents hard against the screaming white, white wall.

Mindful of the better part of valour, Harrison retreated to his inner office and dialled a number.

* * *

"Perfection," murmurs Dr. Sijkzak. "You were talking about perfection."

Araminta sighs. This is not proving to be a productive encounter from either side. He has been telling her that she is menopausal, *ver-eee* menopausal, that women of her age often lose confidence, feel themselves lacking, feel even that they have failed in some way.

"It can be very hard to accept that you can no longer be what you were But once you have come to terms with it, embraced it, even, you will experience a new peace of mind, one that now seems impossible. That will be your own, individual perfection."

Bullshit, thinks Araminta Winter-Clive, sitting bolt upright upon her perfect buttocks and nosing her pointed breasts more aggressively at him. Dr. Sijkzak feels discomfited, not a sensation usual to him.

"Perfection," says Araminta, "is an illusion. It cannot exist. And yet, Harrison strives for it. I have striven for it, trying to keep up with what he wants of me." A brief pause. Then: "And, if I'm honest, what I've wanted for myself."

"And you feel you have failed?" prompts Dr. Sijkzak, the gold rimmed spectacles glinting. Now the discussion can be pulled back onto its proper lines.

"No I bloody have not." Araminta's forthright northern alter ego rears up, aka the self of the three-bedroomed semi and the mediocre comprehensive. "That's the problem. I've succeeded. I am the perfect woman for Harrison Clive and I don't like it. It's not what I wanted."

Dr. Sijkzak, psychiatrist to the rich, the famous and the rich and famous, considers for a moment this astonishing speech. Anyone who does not want to be Harrison Clive's wife is surely deranged. He even fancies this prospect himself, a thought which does not in the least trouble him. We are, after all, every one of us bisexual at base, multi-gender; it is what Nature intended for our biology, so that the species can adapt its urges to the needs of the epoch.

He wonders, in fact, whether a slight but unmistakable schizophrenia is setting in – the *divided self,* not uncommon at this stage of life – perhaps a mid-life paranoia? He reaches cautiously for his prescription pad in its platinum holder.

"And what did, or do you want out of life, Mrs. Clive?"

The platinum pen moves rapidly over the thick, creamy parchment.

"Kids,"says Araminta succinctly. "A floppy bust. Shitty nappies. Bread rising in the oven. Friends stopping by for a coffee, not expecting a cordon bleu dinner. Toys on the floor to fall over. Muddle. Grandchildren in an untidy garden. Grey hair and a big, toddler-friendly lap."

The pen moves faster. Clearly this woman is critical.

"Above all –" Araminta stands up – "I want to be myself."

"Ah." Sensing with relief the end of a trying hour, Dr. Sijkzak smooths his dark, sleek hair and looks up at his client. "But do you know what that is?"

He hands her a folded piece of parchment with its indecipherable, doctor's scrawl.

"Not any more," retorts Araminta, tearing the paper into confetti bits, "but as Harrison might say, I aim to find out."

* * *

It is afternoon in the jungle. Araminta and Harrison Clive are on safari (if one can borrow the expression and re-locate it in South America).

It is her idea, and because Harrison has learned to love her, and because he cannot be bothered not to, he has given in to it. After all, why not? She has been so much better recently, sleeping soundly, fucking vigorously with the sort of energy she used to have. And they are neither of them getting any younger, so why not have some adventure whilst they still can?

Thus they have come to this South American country, these two lightly tanned, sturdy, middle-aged wealthy Europeans, to get some new experience. The route to where they are right now has been arduous and trying; Araminta insists they do it all by jeep. They camp, they stay in small towns, and then villages, and then huddles of huts, and they hire a native guide. He is cheerful, neat, clean and a good cook; he has passable English. He is also totally uncynical and regards his charges with affection and pride. Mrs. Clive is a wonderful lady, albeit nearly twice his height

Harrison has been bitten by something and his face has come up red and blotchy. There is no ointment left to soothe it. He is growing a beard and this is not right now at its most picturesque, nor is it comfortable. His digestion is playing up a little. But he's still enjoying himself. It is – different. He has always liked different, providing that he can end the experience at any time. And he has the money to fly himself right out of here if it gets worse.

Araminta is taking it all in her stride. Insects do not attack the perfected flesh, perhaps aware of the silicone only a millimetre under the smooth surface. She eats well and suffers nothing. (All that saved three-weeks-old custard, a lifetime's guarantee against gastroenteritis.) She sleeps well, whereas poor Harrison mutters, groans and scratches feebly at himself in his hammock. Sexually she has found new verve and abandonment, and batters his tender body in the long hot afternoons when they are supposed to be resting. The native guide fishes, whittles wood, sits in his tent a way off, and envies Harrison Clive.

Moreover, it has to be said that Araminta's hair has grown longer, rougher, and is reverting to that dried-out blonde of her earlier years, this time without the help of the little bottles. The expensive honey tones do not take long to disappear.

They trek deeper into the jungle, the jeep abandoned

now, the journeying by foot. It is unbelievably hot, sultry, steamy, and there are snakes and God knows what else in the undergrowth. But Harrison is still enjoying it. Truth to tell, he rather likes this new (or renewed) Araminta that forges ahead of him, that straddles him dominatrix style in the tent and pumps her heavy-muscled body up and down, the sharp breasts bruising his helpless nose.

Further they go, until all they find are tiny settlements where the people live in tribal clusters, eat only what they find around them and are amazed by huge blonde Araminta, by smoothly brown, bristly Harrison and even by the sophisticated native guide who can speak this ugly, strange language.

Finally, they reach the ultimate spot of their trip.

"We can go no further," says the guide. "Even jungle people will not go upon that mountain."

"Well I want to," says Araminta Winter (Clive), peering at the mysterious, gaunt bluish purple peak beyond.

"Don't be silly, honey," says Harrison, who has acclimatised somewhat. His guts are settling, his face subsiding, his beard is established and trimmed daily, and he's encouraged by the thought that this is the half-way point. By this, he means that they will now turn back. It has been a wonderful experience, and he will have a lot of incredible stories to tell them all back home in Spain, in California, in New York, in London, and even on that Scottish island (with sufficient Scotch). He might even write a book about it, and pay a top publisher to take it.

But his beloved stands there amidst the massive-leafed, sweating trees, amidst the raucous, riotous birds and the staring villagers. She regards the native women thoughtfully. Bare-breasted, with little loin cloths wrapped briefly round their waists, they swing their sticks to grind the food, walk with lopping bosoms as they load their children easily on their hips, their breasts hanging, swaying, asserting their right to be there, sagging or not sagging, just emphatically to be.

Araminta utters a strange yell, a cross between triumph and sudden self-realisation as in a flash of exploding inner light, and strips off her safari shirt, her cunningly moulded lightweight tropical brassiere, and lets herself fall free, unrestrained amongst all the beautiful, pendulous dark breasts of the women around her. She sniffs deeply of the sticky, moist hot air and sets off with purpose towards the narrow track ahead.

Harrison and the Indian guide move hastily towards her, Piti with a covering cloth. But Araminta brushes them aside. With head held high, like the woman who carries a great bundle on her slim, strong neck, she marches on through the low dense foliage, pushing aside the succulent leaves, the myriad insect life, taking those two perfect, pointed, eternally thrusting and expensive breasts before her.

LUCIA

MIGUEL ROLLED OVER onto his young, strong back; reached for the packet of cigarettes beside the bed. Always, afterwards, straight away, a cigarette – or two, perhaps. They did this in the movies.

He lit up; took a long, thirsty drag, exhaled a gush of smoke between his heavy, full lips, stared at the ceiling. He did not look at the lissom, long-haired girl beside him. Had not looked at her much, all the way through. Why now?

Impatient, the girl sighed; her lips parted, though not in desire.

"She wants her meal now," Miguel grumbled to himself.

Prolonging the moment of pure, unspoiled male selfishness, Miguel lounged on his back, pulling on the cigarette to the very last of the butt, whilst the girl picked restlessly at the crumpled sheet around them.

Suddenly, Miguel had had enough. Rapidly, with a start of energy surprising in his lumbering frame, he got up from the bed, thrust on his jeans and sweatshirt, turned briefly to the girl and gave her a nod.

"It's late," he said, abrupt, cold. "Let's go and eat."

The girl rose, dressed quickly, and dragged a comb through her dense, tousled hair, applied lipstick to the well-shaped mouth. Together, they made a curious pair: Miguel clumsily crafted, loutish; she finer of feature, pretty in the way that Andalusian pueblo girls are, with the supple body that would, in times gone by, in her grandmother's day, have flattened and sagged with the effort of relentless child bearing and the ceasing of passion; perhaps not so nowadays, but still a possibility.

Her name, as it happened, was Carmelita, but this was unimportant. She was one of a string of girls that Miguel somehow managed to attract, albeit as a rule briefly. There would be a curious, hypnotic flirtation, in which his natural coarseness would be subdued; he could play the gentleman, the Don Juan, even, for a while. There might be a couple of red roses pushed shyly onto the girl's doorstep at night. Then, sometimes, a full sexual encounter, but in a place sufficiently far from Miguel's own pueblo for the gossip not to get around; and in any case, even in these days, girls do not give themselves freely. In particular they do not give themselves to an affianced man, a fact that Miguel did not attempt to keep hidden, not out of a sense of caution or delicacy, but because he failed to see that it would be significant.

So, the little dalliance would run its course, it would just as suddenly fizzle out, and Miguel would return to the safety of his street corner bar, and the corner seat with his fiancee, the plump and docile Lucia.

But it was not the anger of Lucia that Miguel feared; she was plain, placid, and in his opinion fairly stupid. This suited him well. More to the point, she was lucky to have him, that was clear; and so she must put up with what Miguel handed out. Rather, he feared the wrath of some other girl's sweetheart, or father, or brother... and thus he kept the more daring of his exploits at a sound geographical distance, travelling the rough, steep roads easily in the darkness on his little sputtering motorcycle machine.

Carmelita had put the finishing touches to her makeup, had given her rounded rump a last, approving look in the smeary mirror behind the door, and stood tapping her high-heeled shoe impatiently. It was clear that they both wanted to get this part of the thing over and done with.

"Out," said Miguel, tersely, opening the door and going through it first. The girl followed, clattering along behind him in her ridiculous heels.

"Wait," she complained. "You go too fast for me."

Reluctantly, Miguel slowed down. Carmelita caught up with him, shot him a curious, sideways smile.

"Do you always treat your women like this?"

"Like what?" Miguel was perplexed. What could she mean? How else did one treat a woman one had just been in bed with?

"Never mind." Carmelita pursed her red, red lips. "Let us talk about something else."

Miguel sighed, looking down at the dark head beside him. He felt obliged to make conversation with this girl. With Lucia, there was no such requirement. She did not have a lot to talk about, and he could sit with her in companionable silence in their corner of the bar, whilst she sipped her one drink of the evening, leaving her fiancee free to rove amongst his friends if he wished, or to let his eye wander to the lusher young women who passed through.

Sometimes there would be a little dancing, if Jose opened up his back room and there was some kind of celebration, and then Miguel might occasionally pair off with one of these young women, lumping her round the floor in a heavy-footed if rhythmic version of dance. Lucia would simply sit in her accustomed place, watching with her vacant smile, much as a mother observes her toddler at play; Miguel would always come back to her.

"What are you thinking of?" Carmelita turned her small, intense face up to his "You're very quiet."

Miguel sighed again. All right, if Carmelita really wanted to know what was in his thoughts, she could have it.

"I was thinking of my fancee."

"Your fiancee?" Carmelita was not so much startled as put out; her lips pouted, the vivid face slumped into a sulk. "You did not tell me you were engaged."

"Why should I?" Miguel was irritated by this line of discussion. "It was nothing to do with you."

"Oh no?" The girl's dark eyes flashed. "Maybe I wouldn't have gone to bed with you if I'd known you had a girl friend."

"Well, you did fuck with me, and you didn't take much persuading," replied Miguel with a sneer. "So perhaps it wouldn't have made much difference anyway. I got the impression you were hot for it. Come on, let's eat. I'm hungry."

Carmelita stood still, her noisy heels silenced on the stones of the street; put her hands on her curving hips; puckered up her mouth again and regarded Miguel shrewdly, as one who is well used to weighing up the peculiarities of men.

"I should slap your face for that remark," she observed, "but instead, I will make you suffer for it."

And she laughed, showing a set of perfect, slightly pointed white teeth. In the semi-dark she looked like a young hyena, and Miguel involuntarily shivered.

"It's cold out here," he said, to cover the moment. "Get into the bar."

"Okay," said Carmelita. "But let's at least go and eat as friends. I won't have a meal with someone who is my enemy."

"Don't be silly." Miguel was bored now. "Of course we are friends. We're just being honest with each other – not always pleasant."

"Kiss me, then, if we are friends."

Casting his eyes heavenwards, Miguel made to step into the cafe-bar, from whence a good smell of food was wafting across his face.

"I shall scream and tear my blouse if you don't."

Hastily, remembering those hyena teeth, Miguel reached for the girl, took her warm, gently ripening body to him and kissed her full on the mouth, wetly and without finesse. He found it agreeable. Carmelita drew back, and gave him a narrow smile. Without another word, she led the way into the bar, and Miguel was further dismayed to notice that she tucked her arm through his, nestling into him in a way that was unmistakably possessive. Often at this stage the girl in question was as tired of the whole thing as he; he hoped that this was not one of the unusual ones who wanted to go on seeing him. Occasionally they did; some were attracted by a certain oafish, adolescent quality, a direct and frank declaration of self-interested sexual intent.

Besides, Miguel was tall, and though cast on the bulky mould, not ill shaped; had rough, black hair, worn slightly longer and curlier than most; good, well set eyes in an otherwise full jowled face. He was a little different, somehow, than other young men of the pueblos, and this gave him the air of having qualities undefined but intriguing. In fact, it was merely the charisma of arrogant, heedless youth and the self-seeking energy that goes with it; Miguel would find his charms, such as they were, on the wane well before he was thirty.

"Go and sit over there," he ordered, disengaging the entwined arm and pushing thr girl in the direction of a free table.

He thought wistfully of Lucia. He had a sort of unwilling, beast-like fondness for her, born of the familiarity bred by twenty-two years of shared childhood in a small, inland mountain village. A match between them, approved in principle long ago by their parents, in houses on opposite sides of the street, was a natural progression from their days playing in the large gang of neighbouring children, when Miguel would mock Lucia for her rabbit teeth and her plumpness, but fiercely beat up anyone from another street who insulted her. Their marriage would be the logical conclusion of such a long-standing loyalty between families, amongst people of a *barrio*.

He glanced across at the sinuous Carmelita, now sitting expectantly with legs crossed to display them to their best advantage. Something about her made him nervous; not a feeling to which Miguel was accustomed. To his further discomfort, she managed to sit very close to him as they ate their meal, periodically reaching out to squeeze his hand.

"Don't do that," he said, sharply. "We are not really – an item, are we?"

The girl flushed, and frowned.

"That silly fiancee of yours," she murmured. "Why don't you break with her? If she's a pueblo girl from the mountains, she must be a good breeding cow. She'd soon find someone else."

"Shut up!" Miguel's voice came out in a hiss, and he kicked Carmelita's ankle under the table. "Lucia is my fiancee and she is a good girl. In June I shall marry her."

The girl sulked.

"And continue to see others, to be unfaithful, to sleep around? As you do at present? Is that what you want?"

"That is not your business," retorted Miguel, stiffly. "Eat up, and I will take you home. It is late."

The meal was finished in silence, but despite himself, Miguel dwelt on what Carmelita had said. Lately, he had begun to be less careful in his adventurings. There had been a couple of occasions when he had even left their own street corner bar with some girl, his arm brazenly curled round a narrow waist, hand spreading down to the undulating, pear heavy hips. Still Lucia's expression of bovine calm had not changed, even if Miguel was out of the bar for as much as an hour. It had not previously crossed Miguel's mind to wonder what Lucia might be thinking, after these short episodes of back street groping and quick, over the clothes satisfaction. He always went back to her, he would oblige her sufficiently when the time came, so that there would be ninos. Was that not enough?

Now, with this girl, these thoughts disturbed him, and in a split second of rare self-doubt, he looked up from his dinner and caught Carmelita's eye. It was predatory.

Seeing – and seizing – her chance, Carmelita slipped her hand, with its vermilion, clawed nails, onto Miguel's thigh. He was reminded of what those nails had done to him in bed.

"I wish," she said on a long, plaintive breath, "I wish you would stay with me tonight."

The hand slid subtly up his leg, each talon digging in on its way. Carmeita's bright, dark face came close to his, her mouth slightly open.

Miguel felt the desire rise in him again like a hot tide. To hell with Lucia for tonight! She never complained about anything, and she must know; she was not entirely dense. In any case, what was the problem? He would not shame Lucia before they were married – she was, it went without saying, a virgin. Miguel had never felt moved to enact with her more than a few light kisses and some mild cosseting of her full, tightly-bound breasts, which Lucia permitted; below her already wide waist was a mystery to Miguel and remained Lucia's secret. They were barrio families, as good as related, and it would not go down well if she were to be embarrassed by the time her wedding day arrived.

Besides, there was no need. Miguel found what he wanted in his sporadic, furtive couplings with the sharper, more modern girls in the distant towns, who also took from him the burden of responsibility. Lucia would, beyond a doubt, become pregnant in the first two months of their marriage; he had no intention of saddling himself with the complex matter of preventing it.

Having thus freed himself of the inconvenient, and quite out-of-the-way twinges of guilt, Miguel succumbed to the more familiar urges arising from Carmelita's attributes.

* * *

Two weeks, three weeks, almost a month later and Miguel was still seeing her. It was not that he was in love – there was only one love object in his life, and that was himself – but he found the girl hard to resist. For one thing, there was a toughness about her, a self-engrossed sensualit, a determination to seek her own pleasure equalling his own, and for another, their physical encounters were becoming more spectacularly gratifying by the week.

She would ask him about Lucia, though. At first he was loath to talk about his fiancee, out of some dim feeling that one should not mix two worlds and that it was improper; but later he found himself speaking more freely.

"But do you love her?" insisted Carmelita one night, running those agonisingly pleasurable talons straight down his torso.

"Well." Miguel paused. Carmelita evoked complete honestly, in her direct, female, demanding way. "I suppose you can call it love. I have known her a long time, since we were kids. It is a sort of love."

"And that is enough to marry someone?"

"Marriage does not concern love. It is to do with family relationships, convenience, the having of children."

"What a load of shit!" Carmelita shook her long dark curls in contempt. "This is the modern age. You should be free to choose – out of love."

Miguel shrugged. Such questions did not interest him.

"We have seen each other every Saturday, and sometimes an evening in between, for eight years now," he said, but the words sounded lame and left his mind (not used to a great deal of speculative activity) discomposed.

Indeed, he continued to take Lucia to the pueblo bar on Saturday evenings; even asked her to dance with him once, there being no young women to catch his eye. By this time, though he either did not know it or buried his head so that he did not hear, rumours were beginning to travel as far as the village. Tongues were telling of Miguel and the girl – the same girl, mark you – he had been seen with in a certain town. Soon, the reports spread beyond the street, rippling out from the stone that had been so carelessly tossed into it – the news of Miguel's continuing infidelity to Lucia.

Hitherto, his half-hearted peccadilloes had been ignored, much as Lucia herself ignored them; even regarded with disdain. But this was a different matter, of a different order of things, and the tongues clicked their disapproval in harsh syllables that echoed in the courtyards, flung from one wash balcony to another, and ricocheted off the white, glaring walls in the quiet of the afternoon siesta, to rattle and whisper into Miguel's head during his dreams like a small spray of pebbles thrown against his window, making him turn and mutter in his sleep. Only Miguel's fiancee remained unmoved, silent.

Thus the street held its breath, people reined in their

impulses, taking their lead from the stolid Lucia.

One Saturday, Miguel asked her, as one tempting the Fates might do, if she realised that he was seeing another girl.

"I have heard some things," said Lucia mildly.

Miguel found it difficult to say more but eventually, out of a sort of idle curiosity, he said,

"Don't you mind?"

There was another pause. Then,

"It's not a question of whether I mind," replied Lucia, "but of whether you do."

This unexpected sophistication, this ambiguity, was a shock; he had not learned to associate subtlety with Lucia. To whom had she been talking, to come up with such an idea? He looked more closely at her, but she only smiled in that vacant, amiable way, her round, light brown eyes fixed expressionlessly on his face.

Nonplussed, and for want of knowing what to say next, Miguel put his arm round his fiancee and kissed her, hard and full, on the mouth. Suddenly, he desired her very strongly; sexuality was running high in him these days, and in a month she would be his bride. He forgot that they were in the public view in Jose's bar, and groped for her breast, covering the fullness with his large hand, grasping it as if holding on for his life. His other hand fumbled with the bottom of her skirt.

"Lucia!" he grunted.

There was a a stinging, deafening blow to his left ear. Dazed, Miguel released the breast, sat back and clutched his head. He looked at his fiancee, but she was sitting as calmly as ever, merely gazing at a point behind him. With a premonition tickling the back of his neck, Miguel turned and saw Carmelita, hands on tightly-skirted hips in that characteristic posture of hers, her taut little face full of fury.

"Swine!" she hissed. "How can you make love to that – that fat sow? Is this the girl you told me you would marry? What in hell do you see in her? Eh?"

In derisive venom she turned her attention to the un-blinking Lucia.

"You stupid bitch! Do you think you will keep your Miguel, when the only reason he stays with you is for your father's money?"

Lucia appeared untouched, her countenance as stone. Carmelita pushed her vixen-face closer, into the other girl's, and spat.

"I will take him from you before you know what is hap-pening! When Miguel and I are in bed together he forgets all about you, oh yes, he forgets it all. He only comes back to you out of duty, and soon I'll make him forget that too. You are plain and fat, and you'll look old and ugly after your first child. Miguel said so."

On the triumphant last words, Carmelita ground her stiletto heel into the floor as one screwing down a victory, swept round on her tottering shoes and tapped smartly from the bar. There was a hush amongst Jose's custom-ers; then, for Lucia's sake, a tactful, subdued chattering. Miguel, his ear still painful, spread out his hands helpless-ly to the world in general. He looked at Lucia. Her face had not lost its blankness, but from one eye a tear slowly emerged and ran in a sluggish rivulet down her full cheek.

Miguel stood up in horror, backed away from her and edged out of the bar and into the street. He would go for a walk. All this was somewhat beyond him. His head ached, and not only because of the slap he had received. As he plodded dully through the warm night air, his head cleared a little and the appalling mess of his situation rose up before him. Miguel, having created it, was quite un-suited to deal with it, and he wished to be relieved of this as of all other responsibilities in his life. He groaned softly and turned his face to the stars.

"Dear God!" His lips moved in silent prayer. "Father in Heaven, show me the way."

In what might have been immediate response to this pious entreaty, four figures sprang out of the shadows behind Rosa's Merceria (now shuttered and closed for the night) and fell upon Miguel. They were Lucia's oldest brother, Jesus, married at twenty eight with three children and built in the family tradition like a young bullock; her middle brother, Antonio, newly married and expectant and equally covered in flesh and muscle; Lucia's nineteen year old cousin, Pedro, a tall and athletic youth; and an older, widowed uncle from a nearby pueblo whose name eluded Miguel at this critical moment but whom he recalled as having been a prize winning amateur boxer in his youth.

Their business, directly administered and without verbal exchange, was swift, simple and to the point. Miguel struck out feebly in a series of unwieldy, misplaced body punches and aimless swipes, but these were token gestures against the efficient hammer-blows that were delivered systematically to his shoulders, chest, back, ribs, arms and occasionally his nose; somewhere in amongst it there were some spiked kicks up and down his legs. Miguel in blackening confusion suspected Pedro of these last; the youth had recently acquired a pair of somewhat avant garde boots with a lot of metal about them.

The gang of four were careful, however, not to inflict damage to Miguel's skull; they did not want a vegetable as an in-law; and they left his genitals alone. They wanted offspring from this union, preferably male. Every other part of Miguel was an open target, and as he sank into a painfully achieved oblivion against Rosa's shop doorway, Miguel knew that in more than one sense he was done for.

* * *

It was not until a week before the wedding when, late in the month of June, Miguel was able to sit once more with Lucia in their place in the bar. Her family had been unwontedly kind to him since he had limped out of his house two days after his assailants had left him in the street to sort himself out.

"We hear you were attacked," they said with faces of moral indignation and righteous horror. "In the name of Mary, what is this place coming to?"

"I understand you have been obligated to take time off work," said Lucia's father. "I will be pleased if you will take this to compensate you in some measure."

Miguel knew that this was an order, not an offer or a request; wordlessly, he took the wad of bills. He also knew that this was an instruction to buy his fiancee gold.

Lucia was allowed to visit him at his parents' home, where Miguel's father, surly, and his mother, shamefaced, had made awkward hosts. Lucia herself had been as usual – serene, affectionate, and perhaps a little more communicative, informing him of plans for the wedding and the gifts they had received.

On this evening, near to their nuptial feast, Miguel sat in broody silence and nursed his still healing bruises. Even had he been so inclined, he would not have been able to perform outstanding feats of love making tonight. Girls, swinging-hipped, long haired, bright eyed, came and went in the bar; there was dancing in the back room.

"Hey, Miguel" You don't dance?"

"What are you looking so miserable about? Go and join the fun!"

Miguel winced as Jose waved his tray of glasses expertly close to his aching shoulders. He eyed the throng of girls morosely, firmly pinned by his damaged body and a newly installed conscience to his fiancee's side. She, Lucia, sat as always, sipping her modest drink slowly and ruminatively, her face displaying her customary calm, nothing more.

All at once, Carmelita came into the bar. She was not of this area, and had not been seen since the night of Miguel's nemesis. Features turned down in lip curling scorn, she glanced briefly in their direction. Lucia's habitually dormant eyes gleamed with a sudden heat. As Carmelita passed very near to them, swirling her new gypsy skirt and setting her outsize silver earrings jangling (they had rewarded her well), Miguel's fiancee lifted her head high and in a self-conscious gesture, put her left hand on his thigh. The small diamond in her ring flashed and sparkled in the disco light.

Tossing back her braids of hair, Carmelita sashayed through to the dance floor, escorted by a slender, eager youth, his hand planted firmly on her satined backside.

Miguel's head drooped; his spirits drooped. All of him drooped. He did not think he would be capable of making love to any woman again. The dull years of faithful matrimony stretched out ahead of him like an endless, grey road.

Lucia smiled; a rare, wide smile as the sun after a storm parts the bloated clouds. She looked proudly around her. She was in her place in the bar, with her fiance. He was hers. Soon, very soon, he would be her husband.

ONE DAY

THIS IS A STORY that could be set anywhere, in almost any place in the world. There is no reason that I should give it a definitive location, or, indeed, give my characters particular names. It is one of the many variations on the old theme – Man and Woman – and we could say it is in France, or England, Chile, or even Japan; and I could call my characters Yvette, John, Pablo, Yoko, or what have you.

But for the sake of convenience, and so that your thoughts might roost somewhere, I am going to say that it is in Italy that our protagonist lives, and where his adventure takes place. For Italian is the language of love, is it not, and are the Italians not the most romantic on earth? Well, so they so; and it will do.

Let us imagine a small town in the north of Italy, where the mountains rise impressive but distant, and where the trees stand stiffly, dark green; and where the men are occupied by day in the industries that clutter the plains and by night in the usual male pursuits of drinking, talking politics, maybe giving their expert views on the football – oh, and love.

My hero is going to be called Guiseppe, and he works in a car factory. "Not very romantic," I hear you mutter. Well, no. But my Guiseppe has a bold heart. He is young – say twenty-four – and he sings as he works; not the classical pieces of the opera, of course, but the more popular airs of light romance with much trilling, con *molto sentimento*. It is a happy sound that he makes; he has a sweet if slightly theatrical baritone and he is quite handsome of feature. I can see you ask a question: this paragon of all the male virtues must surely be married, or at least on the way to the church door? Now I must confess to you, draw the last detail out of the bag; reluctantly, I tell you that our Guiseppe is very, very short in stature. Not a dwarf, you understand, but small enough to make him one of those suitors whom prospective mothers-in-law (and their more modern daughters) consider and put aside, mentally reserving him in case all else fails. He is, if you like, the male wallflower of the dating game. Nobody, after all, wants to breed sons of a mere metre and a half if they can avoid it.

However, Guiseppe's work mates smile as they listen to him, and the women who work in the offices roll their eyes at him as they pass. His mother thinks he is wonderful, come straight from the lap of God into her blessed womb, and frets not a little as the years go by and her son shows no interest in pursuing a courtship. There are, by now, a few marriageable maidens not yet taken up; there is Sylvie Leone, who admitted has a strong squint and exceptionally large ears, but is a good honest girl; there is Paulina Travolta, who missed the boat a few years ago by playing fast and loose, but who has now settled down and even is she has a Past, for sure she will behave herself now if she gets a late chance; there is also Anna Morena, who is well over thirty but who would make a good wife, despite her real handicap of standing at a metre eighty; and then, lastly, we have little Cecilia Forte, as lacking in height as is Giuseppe himself – what could be more ideal? Giuseppe's mama will concede that none of these ladies seems in the least interested in her angelic son, Cecilia having a perverse predilection for very tall men; but surely, if Giuseppe were to show himself a little more willing, something could be managed? Mama heaves a long, tragic sigh, and mops away the moisture at her eyes; in the back of her mind there is a nasty, creeping thought like a skinny worm, and she crosses herself hastily to drive it away.

But Giuseppe's mother need not worry. Her son has all the proper, masculine instincts and inclinations. The fact is, he has a secret, though not the one his mother fears. He has fixed his interest a long time ago, almost in childhood when he and his big sisters and his many cousins would play in the orchards and chase each other in and out of the dappled light, dodging and ducking under low branches, swinging beneath the heavy apples and plums and like the fruit falling at last into the sweet, dry grass in a merry heap, tumbling, laughing and brown. Giuseppe would like there, breathing harshly like a well-worked pony, delirious with chasing and running, and then he would look up into the mature, sensual face of his cousin Francesca; and she would stare down at him, little cousin Giuseppe, small but very cute, and three years younger; and they would grow serious, with only the sound of the others' laughter in their ears, far off. Those were the remembered summers of his youth, and Giuseppe has nurtured his dream ever since.

And all these years later, Francesca is a comely, melon-breasted, wasp-waisted young woman with endless, shapely legs on which she stands – alas! – so much taller than he. (When she does wear her highest heels, Giuseppe can only crane his neck to gawp upwards, as one might standing under Pisa.) Francesca of the olive skin and the cat's green eyes and the tawny, uneven folds of hair that cascade all about her slender neck and curving shoulders, to trickle finally down her smooth, supple back to the delicious, undulating rump... Francesca walks barelegged barefoot in the summer, with freedom in her stride and liberty in her heart. It is the freedom of the young widow; married at eighteen, a son at twenty, bereaved at twenty-two before she had time properly to know her man, Francesca now has the comfortable status of the widowed woman, coupled with a knowledge of married sex in all its diversity, no longer in doubt and with plenty of time. No wonder she is so confident as she swings along in her token black, the V-line sweater deeply revealing the lush swell of breasts, the short skirt merely brushing the smooth, golden thighs... Giuseppe, the defender of the family reputation, its honour, wishes his cousin wouldn't dress like this. What will people think? Giuseppe the besotted, Giuseppe the would-be lover, is glad that she does. Oh, Francesca!

She has many admiriers, it goes without saying, this wondrous cousin; but she is in no hurry to make her choice. She has also made it clear that when – and if – she chooses to remarry, it will not be to Giuseppe.

"They would think I was on honeymoon with my kid brother!"

She laughs, and teases his hair. Giuseppe flushes and wishes she wouldn't. People will see. Oh please do it again, Francesca!

"Cousin!"

Giuseppe decides it is not a good idea to go down on one knee – enough lack of stature is enough, when all is said and done – and contents himself with a hand flung hopelessly on his stricken heart.

"Cousin, beautiful, adorable Francesca, I know that I can never hope to make you mine, but oh, I would give anything, all I have, all you can name, merely to possess you once – just once!"

"Only once, eh?"

Francesca's green eyes narrow and blink like a cat's in the sun. "Are you sure? That doesn't sound very passionate. Most men want me for more than a quick once, little Giuseppe"

96

"No, no!" Giuseppe is frantic to make her understand. "Francesca, I know only too well that I am not the man you would choose, I know I am small and therefore ridiculous, I know I can never hope to be anything more to you than absurd little cousin Giuseppe – therefore, to be able to make love to you for just one time, to have you for my own even for so fleeting a moment, oh it would be, how can I say, oh Francesca – "

"Well." Francesca listens to this rapid torrent, puts her head on one side in squinting scrutiny. "That's a modest request, I must say, very modest."

She pauses. Giuseppe holds his breath whilst she considers him again, at length, the vivid eyes scanning him from his the top of his curly-haired crown, down to his quite broad shoulders, taking in the flawless light Italian skin, seems to note his neat waistline (he goes to the gym), sighs briefly over the lilliputian legs. He is on the rack. His nails are in shreds, his teeth in danger of being ground to powder. Francesca, please!

His cousin puts her golden-olive face very close to his, the eyes glinting, the full lips brushing his ear and he hears her words through a fog of vertigo as the blood pounds in his head and his knees betray him so that he has to sit down abruptly, or risk the further indignity of a faint.

"If I could have your solemn word that it would be only on that one occasion, then I daresay that one day – I would not like to say when, mark you – one day it could be possible."

And with a wide grin, a toss of her sun-streaked hair and a swirl of the short, flaring skirt, she is off down the hill to the market, where the stalls have been doing brisk business since early morning; where overripe fruit and stray vegetables have been sturdily trampled underfoot and where the vendors are now desperate to sell and are out-shouting each other noisily and cheerily to announce their crashing prices. Last bargains! Last few left!

Released fro his torment, Giuseppe lets out a long, slow exhalation and wanders slowly downhill to the cacophony below. His heart soars. She will never want him for more, of course; how could he expect it? (Giuseppe is not a vain man, his extreme diminutiveness and years of playground mockery saving him from the worst excesses of character in the Italian male.) But just once, to have her, wholly, freely, giving herself to him, abandoning herself to his every desire... He stands for a moment in the sunny street, in his own oasis of quiet, contemplating this incredible vision. Spreads out his broad, powerful workman's hands in supplication. Dear Mother of God, prays Giuseppe in genuine reverence, let this miracle be! Let me know the softness of those divine breasts, oh forgive me for the blasphemy, sweet Mother of Jesus, but indeed they are! Let me find, just once, the secret she keeps between those heavenly – oh pardon me, our Lady of God!

And so on, and so forth.

There is a lot more of this sort of thing, but I don't intend to bore you with it, so let your reader's eye wander from our hero, leave him in his reverential ecstasy, and rather turn to the raucous, milling market, riotous with the hues of red, green and orange capsicum and purple swollen aubergines; the all-coloured fruits and the huge lettuce, radish, corn bigger than you ever saw in your life; the mounds of sweet biscuits, cakes, nuts and lush dried figs glistening richly and darkly in the diffused sun ; the busy butcheries where meat is sliced chopped diced torn ripped shredded minced and parcelled up, all in a trice, and you marvel that this woman's hands once cradled a newborn; and amidst this the dusty black figures of the housewives as they dart from stall to stall to grab their prizes. Younger women stand around in their bright dresses and skin tight jeans with babies latched onto their side-slung hips, chatting amiably in the shoving and the jostling while their older children are given fattening and mouth-rotting sweetmeats by the indulgent traders of the market.

Somewhere here is Francesca, moving easily with her accustomed confident stride through the crowded alleys to make her purchases, those long browned legs carrying her gracefully to the exit, where she turns, spies her cousin at the other end, waves, mouths a "Ciao!" at him, and disappears.

Gisuseppe, immobile, bemused, is brought back to reality with a heavy green thud. It is a cabbage, delivered unceremoniously into his slack hand by the fat stall holder.

"A cabbage for your mamma, Giuseppe. Signora Rossi, she likes a good cabbage, no?"

Giuseppe stands dumbly nodding, whilst the smiling ladies regard him kindly.

"Hey! When will you be getting married, Giuseppe? Time you got yourself settled down, eh?"

"Ah, the small ones always go last. Same with cabbages, same with men!"

And he lingers there in the market, as if to savour the last perfumed traces of Francesca, savouring his moment, clutching this earthly lump which could so easily have been her breast, his feet planted squarely in a carpet of multi-coloured decaying matter and his soul on wings. The mingled pain and joy of such a promised encounter with Francesca is almost too much to bear, and so he stumbles homeward with his prosaic burden, to be to his mamma what he always is – the conscientious, loving, only son.

* * *

We next see Francesca about a month later, at her sister's wedding. It is a big, family affair of course, and one can catch only passing glimpses of her amongst the chattering throng of relations from both sides of the family. How beautiful she looks! How infinitely desirable! How she quite outshines the little bride, this Francesca, in her knee-length dress of black lace, a fine black shawl thrown demurely over her head and shoulders for the church. Later, the shawl slips to the floor, unheeded, and Giuseppe's heart thuds as the pure lines of her neck, the taut swelling of upper bosom are revealed to his parched gaze. Mesmerised, he takes another long swig of refreshing wine as a man crawls for the water jar in the desert.

Later, when some of the relations have at last decided to take their leave, when the eating and drinking have slid one day into the early hours of the next and the bridal couple, now forgotten, have long departed for the package-holiday honeymoon, Giuseppe slips out in the small, dark yard outside Francesca's parents' house.

A voice startles him.

"Well, cousin," says Francesca, slightly mocking as she leans casually against the cool, greyish, limed wall, "and do you still think of me sometimes?"

In the musky night air, in the dimness of the yard lit only by a shadowed moon, Giuseppe can just make out the silvered frame of Francesca's face and her strange, glinting eyes. She flashes him her smile, and puts a hand to her silhouetted neck. He can see the outline of the full bosom heaving gently, as if its owner is mildly breathless.

"Ah, Francesca," he groans, "all the time! You never leave my thoughts, you are always in my heart. When will you be mine?"

(The reader must be indulgent: Giuseppe is a man of cliché. Not a stupid one, I would not want you to think

100

that; but his thoughts run on simple lines, and to the point. Not a bad thing: maybe. But remember, clichés are apt to ensnare the one who thinks by them.)

In the silence provided by these notions, Francesca eyes him dispassionately. In the faint light, you might make out just a gleam of amusement, of irony, in her brilliant eyes, in the hastily covered, brief smile.

She moves away from him, putting herself into an area of direct moonlight, as the clouds part; and slowly, deliberately, unfastens the tiny, covered buttons at the top of her black lace dress. The swelling breasts thrust roundly into Giuseppe's vision; one button, two; two buttons, three; four and five... almost, nearly, but not quite to the button-like nipples.

"Ah, it's so hot!" sighs Francesca on a husky outbreath. "Little cousin aren't you hot?"

"H-hot?" yammers Giuseppe, his loins in turmoil. "Francesca – please – now – just once, only this once -"

And he reaches for her, for that water jar in the desert that quenches the thirst, but she leans imperceptibly further away, her hand searching out the cooling green vine which straggles the rotting trellis. Giuseppe sways clumsily across the uneven paving, clutches her waist and roughly pulls her to him. Francesca is stretching up for the vine, rising on her high heeled shoes; Giuseppe is far below, and so it is not the soft, full lips that offer themselves flauntingly to his gaping mouth but the breasts, fuller still and by far the riper.

"Frances-ca!"

The rear door of the house opens with a rickety, violent scraping noise. Light streams rudely across the concrete of the yard. Francesca's father calls again.

"'Cesca! Your mother wants you. Come into the house."

And in a twinkling, as the moon slithers once more

behind the looming cloud, Giuseppe is left with the trellis and the vine, his seeking mouth full of dry leaves that taste like ash. He pants quietly into the dank wall. What did Francesca whisper as the moved limberly from his grasp?"

"You'll have to wait, little cousin, you'll have to wait."

* * *

We might cool down, at this point, and wipe our brows, and pause to speculate what all this is doing to our poor Giuseppe, the leading figure in this heart rending tale. Well, I can tell you that the next few weeks are pure anguish for our man. His thoughts go back and forth like summer mayflies, as quickly dying as they are born. He is sure that Francesca will keep her promise; after all, she did unbutton her top that night in the yard, and she is not the sort of girl to – well, girls in his family don't – do they? Unless? – But again, he is sure she is fond of him, he remembers the times under the apple trees, how she would look down at him and the world would go quiet, and he is fairly certain that she sometimes looks at him that way now; and once, just once, after all, she said so herself, is not so much to ask. But oh! Horrid thought. What if she finds a lover, a new husband, even? Will she then honour her vow? So Giuseppe lurches from anticipation to expectancy, through resignation to faint optimism which drags out painfully into a sort of dull hope. The waiting turns out to be very long; Giuseppe is not really sure whether he can stand it.

Then, one morning, quite unexpectedly he bumps into his cousin on the bus into town. It is a day off for him, and he is taking his mother shopping to the centre, by public transport as driving and parking is a nightmare, and he sees quite enough of autos during his working hours. Francesca is far up the bus and does not see him at once, and so Giuseppe can observe her for some time. She is dressed in her usual black, but presents herself as prim today in a high-necked blouse and a longish, straight skirt. Her hair is drawn back into a severe chignon low on the graceful, arching neck. Her makeup is similarly subdued, and even her eyes look duller, as if someone has turned off a lamp. The whole effect gives her a plaintive appearance which inflames Giuseppe's excitement several fold, her very paleness peculiarly provocative. He wishes to protect her from everything, from life, to take her to some beautiful meadow, to lay her down gently among the flowers and comfort her with his body, and so on, and -

(Look, I did warn you about the tendency to banality. It's no use complaining to me. Let's get on with the story.)

The crowded bus shuffles its contents to admit more passengers, shoving Giuseppe and his mamma further down where Francesca spies them and turns in surprise.

"Aunt Emilia! What are you doing out so early?"

"We might ask the same of you," replies Signora Rossi. "And where is young Vittorio?"

"It is hard!" sighs Francesca. "I have to find a job. My father is not well – he can't work so much now, and so I'm going for an interview at a new hotel today. They want a housekeeper. Vittorio is with mamma. She will take him to school and bring him home."

Giuseppe's tender, afflicted heart swells and swoons at this tragic story. If only... after all, his salary...

But before he can get going on this one, you'll be glad to know, the bus reaches their stop; his mother is already waddling down to the exit doors at the back. He sidles past the sombre Francesca, enjoying the briefest of physical contact with this goddess in human form, and breathes in her ear,

"When, Francesca, when?"

The bus gives a happy little lurch, and for a delicious moment she is pressed against him from bosom through hip to thighs, the whole length in one glorious, unbidden chance.

"Soon!" his cousin whispers on a sigh. "Be patient, little man, be patient." And then, loudly, "Wish me luck, Aunt Emilia."

Giuseppe knows his cue, alights behind his stout mamma, and struggles for the next hour and a half to behave like a normal man, despite the changes in his anatomy and in his overheated brain. His moment is near, she has said so! All things come to he who waits.

But Giuseppe cannot be patient and from this day on, his mere existence becomes one of exquisite torture. From second to second his senses are strained to the ultimate; every passing, wriggling backside recalls Francesca; every pushing haunch reminds him of the unforgettable moment in the bus; every head of swinging, striped, brown-blonde hair is Francesca's. His days and nights are filled with images of her, which grow more daring and explicit with the mounting of his frustrations. He sleeps but poorly, as all such lovers do, and even his mamma notices that he is pale, and has dark circles round his eyes.

"You must stay in your room today, Giuseppe, she declares firmly at last. "You will get sick if you go on like this – you look terrible. Stay in bed and I will make you a good minestrone and bring it up later. Now. Go. Sleep.

Giuseppe protests faintly, but the overpowering, over-loving hand of his mother presses him back onto the tumbled sheets and so, finally, he fratchets himself into a heavy doze. An hour passes; two. Morning turns to heavy mid-day warmth. Giueseppe sleeps, soundly, at last, the kind of rest that has eluded him all these weeks.

The door opens. A faint light steals across the dusty floor. Giuseppe half wakes, startled, fighting the layers of unconsciousness that threaten to drag him down like stones in the sea. A shapely figure in the doorway – certainly not that of his mamma – puts a finger to its lips. Sssshhh!

The figure enters, closes the door silently, tiptoes to the bed. She looks down at him, compassion flooding her lovely face, warming the green eyes to a loving glow. It is Francesca!

Pushing back the rumpled linen, his weariness vanished, Giuseppe sits up. She has come! It is today! With a wild cry he seizes his cousin, flings her unprotesting to the mattress. She gazes up at him adoringly – he is so masterful, so strong, so manly! (Oh, beware! Beware of those rotten clichés, Giuseppe... but no, he does not listen. Well, would you?)

Now Giuseppe flings off his nightshirt tears off her thick black lacy revealing top and oh sweet Jesus oh Our Lady those breasts oh pardon but they are so yes yes he rips at her flimsy brassiere which falls away under the rage of his passion and his mouth is suckling sucking tugging licking his tongue all over her wonderful body she arches her long sinuous back and with one abandoned cry slides off her skirt her tiny hiding-nothing black lace thong and parts her wondrous heavy soft thighs so that Giuseppe can fall gladly thankfully joyfully religiously yes even so bounding between them and he mounts her raises himself above her looks proudly into her slackened face all loose with longing her mouth open in immediate desire her hands reaching for him as he presents her with his stiff massive erect member she moans and moans but no this is Giuseppe's moment he will keep her waiting he plays with her a little rubbing himself up and down her moist thighs and oh Giuseppe she cried oh Giuseppe you great big man I adore you oh take me take me *take* me

and –

rockets and fireworks and thunderbolts are all going off in Giuseppe's head at once this is better than his wildest dreams much much more than he had ever hoped oh praise be to God and dear Mother of our Lord oh let me not burst Giuseppe is going to explode oh take me take implores the weeping Francesca with a triumphant yell Giuseppe aims and victory thrust and –

come Giuseppe come I want you

yes, yes, oh yes

and –

now Giuseppe now come Giuseppe I want you oh yes Francesca oh my darling

but –

Something pops in Giuseppe's head. The voice is shrill. Harsh. Old.

"Giuseppe, come! I want you. Now."

In miserable confusion, Giuseppe floats up from the fog of sleep, clinging to its strands as a poor swimmer grasps the thing that will drown him. His eyes open. He sits up in bed, now properly awake. The room is empty, shuttered dark and silent save for his own laboured breathing. He looks down at himself, at the subsiding tower between his legs. At the floor, where his sweaty nightshirt lies alone.

"Giuseppe, come please! I am calling and calling you!"

It is his mother.

With a weak, despairing groan, naked Giuseppe rolls out of bed and stands on feeble, shaking legs. Hopelessly, forlornly, he pulls at the shrinking organ of his dream; tries a little bucking and pressing against the dressing-table, but to no avail. The poor thing shrivels, ashamed, into its own folds of skin, and hangs limply between his aching testicles.

He opens the bedroom door.

"Mamma?"

She has fallen, heavily, in the hallway. Around her, spilt minestrone soup. Whimpering, Giuseppe drags on a pair of trousers and goes to help his mother. He thinks he will give up religion if the world can be so cruel as this; he will not go to Mass on Sunday but will join the Communist Party instead. He will definitely forsake women forever – except, of course, for his mother. The rest he is going to pass by in the street, without so much as a second glance. He will not support the cause for the continuing emancipation of women (they can stay in the kitchen) and he will no longer give money to the fund for widows and orphans. His heart is steel.

* * *

But of course, dreams and desires do not fade so easily, do not go obediently away as we would will them. Giuseppe is well caught in the mesh of his own imagining, and continues to feel both passion and pain. The spectre of Francesca still haunts him, if not quite as frequently or so intensely. She got the job at the hotel, and now lives in as housekeeper, coming back to her mother's only one day a week; and so he does not see her in the flesh, though the vision of her interrupts him in his waking and sleeping moments as before.

It is about eleven months later that he does, finally meet her again. Suddenly and startlingly, he sees his cousin in a plaza in the town; and for a moment hardly recognises her. She is plumper in the face, though this is not a detraction, and her eyes are again brilliant and alive with a strange luminance that for a moment Giuseppe cannot identify, though he has seen it in women before. Her olive skin glows with a richness that betokens abundant health. Her breasts – those miracles of creation – are fuller than ever, and Giuseppe now sees that on the end of one of them, carelessly open to public view, hangs a clawing and fuzzy-hair infant, which kneads and sucks with an intentness and determination that Giuseppe can only stand and envy. The sight of that dangling, engorged, blue-veined breast is too much for anyone's self-control.

"When, Francesca, when?" he cries, crucified at last by his own need.

Francesca looks up, briefly, from her tiny infant's downy head. Her eyes shimmer at him. Her flopping, untidy hair glistens. She smiles faintly, a dreamy, absorbed, absent-minded, nursing-mother smile.

"One day, Giuseppe," she says comfortably. "One day".

* * *

Here I must leave my poor Giuseppe; there is no point in pursuing his story, for anything – or nothing – could happen now, and there's no telling which

And if you don't like the way it's turned out so far, if you think I've been unfair to my champion, then you are at liberty to change the ending and imagine anything that pleases you more: that Giuseppe did, after all, have Francesca, just that one, that on that one occasion he was Don Juan, Casanova and all the legendary lovers in history combined… For a story does not belong to a writer, once it as left the pen, and it I as much up to you as to me.

But I must point out in defence of the way I have told it that life, sadly, more often comes up as a bitch than a benefactor; that it is more usual for the Giuseppes of this world to be disappointed than not; and that in matters of the heart, Cupid, Eros, takes no heed of justice, abides by no rules, but is ever the trickster who plays us false, most of all in our dreams...

PEARL

"YOU DANCE?"

Pearl looked up, reluctant, dreading. Yes, it was. The funny little man at the back of the bar who had been sending her pleading glances all evening through gold-rimmed glasses perched uncertainly on a bulbous, reddened nose; then there were the tight leather trousers and knitted waistcoat of vaguely Scandinavian design. She had seen him yesterday, when Pearl's one friend here commented with German frankness that even his own mother would have found it hard to love him. *Oh Gudrun*, Pearl said in reproach, feeling the sharp stab of truth. But he had an honest sort of face, like an indeterminate, unwanted dog.

"Well." She hesitated. There was nothing else to do, so – "All right, yes."

They danced. He – Norwegian, convalescing here after "an operation to my heart" – danced badly, holding her to him even in the discotheque numbers, stepping on her feet at each missed beat. Soon, he had to sit down: the heart. His English was execrable, worse than Pearl's Spanish, of which he spoke none.

"What is your name?" she said, and thought that he replied Rudolf. Unfortunate, in view of the nose. But it was Noralf. God knew what that would be in English. Despite the heart, Noralf brought out a pack of twenty international-sized Rothmans, and lit up. He drank rum and coke, with lemon. *Why*, Pearl wondered in silent desperation, *do people do appalling things to themselves and expect to be pitied when their bodies catch up with them?*

But she was stuck with him, damn it. Conversation had to be made. It was tortuous: slow, long pauses, made more difficult by Noralf's insistent mangling of every vowel until it was unrecognisable. She gathered that he had driven from Oslo alone (with the heart?) to Spain for his health. This subject used up most of Noralf's vocabulary, and Pearl began to feel that restless boredom which comes with the awareness that after talking with another for ten minutes you have reached the limits of interest or capacity. What point in continuing? Only a latent politeness, an ancient conditioned courtesy that Pearl could not quite shake off – and a lurking recognition that the alternatives were worse.

What were her choices for the evening? Gudrun was out, meeting her husband at the airport. The short-lived intimacy, of the kind that springs up easily, would now fade just as rapidly. The possibilities, then: to sit alone in the bar, amongst a few dozen elderly sun-seekers, all on the Costa for the winter, no strangers to this tawdry idyll, drinking cheap brandy and ale (which tasted like "nat's piss", the illiterate graffiti in Fuengirola station declared) and performing ritual dances to the terrible music. Pearl would smile sweetly, but this would prove to be a mistake, as they then dragged her protesting to join the Birdie dance in lumbering, heavy-footed rhythm. She would sit down again, flushed and ashamed – of herself, for needing company, any company, at such a price.

But to creep off to her small apartment alone: that was unthinkable. To stare at the striped folk-weave curtains with their ugly, ill-conceived pattern and listen to the endless stream of traffic on the Malaga-Cadiz highway which seemed day and night to be full of expensive fast cars tearing to some exotic place to do exciting things. The lights of the holiday resort, brash, flashy, glared through the unlined folk-weave like a taunt: *We are having a bril-*

liant time! What are you doing, sitting there by yourself?

Pearl started. Noralf had tapped her timidly on the arm, as a mongrel puts its paw on you whilst you're eating your lunch in the park, hoping to be taken home. He had awful teeth, she noticed; uneven, discoloured, full of metal. His breath was a mixture of the vaporous discharges of ill health and stale alcohol.

He leaned towards her, saying something that she could not quite make out. *Would she go out with him, perhaps?* Was that what he was saying?

The breath came strongly across her face and Pearl angled away. For Heaven's sake! She thought. It amazed her continually that men could look so terrible, neglect themselves utterly, and yet feel that they could go in pursuit of a woman, confident as young gods. She, Pearl, lived on the purest food, neither smoked nor drank, her skin was smooth and tanning gently. She was not beautiful, she knew that, but her figure was good and she had a healthy zest. One of those unmarried, good women of the earth, she would look much the same until old age. She had lived sparingly, caring for herself and others in good proportion; but what had it brought her to? A lonely, ailing Norwegian in a run-down Spanish resort, in an apartment block where it was necessary to wash the floor with bleach every day to stem the tides of cockroaches rampant in the plumbing.

Well, thought Pearl, *maybe there's worse than cockroaches.*

The teeth, the breath, were pushing closer to her again; unbearable. Why didn't people engage a good dentist? Why expect others to put up with our mistakes, our flabby, disintegrating selves? Pearl recalled the ageing bodies of the sun-worshippers by the pool, the fried-egg bared breasts of the ladies, brazen here as they wouldn't be at home, the leather wrinkles daily exposed on the sun-beds.

Nudity, like short skirts and broken hearts, belonged to the young. Later, one's body was something to be clothed carefully, papering over the cracks, as it were. Like an old friend, hers had begun to grumble very slightly, a warning to be ever more prudent, more select in the way one lived. If she did not, she and her body fell out every now and then, when hitherto they had got on well.

Oh God. He was asking to see her the next day.

"No," said Pearl, "I am not on holiday. I have to work tomorrow."

Perhaps – the day after? The silly dog, whining faintly, paw scraping.

"Oh, Saturday. I might go to the pool in the afternoon."

Alarm. The soft, wet eyes panicked. He did not bath, he said. "My heart."

Pearl covered her mouth to hide her smile. Really, one must not laugh at the mistakes of someone struggling with an alien language. She did not mean to swim, she told him, rather more kindly. She meant only to lie in the sun.

The moist eyes dried. Ah yes, that would be good. *He could not, you see – with his heart –* he made sweeping, swimming motions and smiled, treating her to more of the metallic teeth.

"You see?" He parted his shirt, baring his pigeon-bowed chest to display a long, angry scar, red and bruised at the edges. Lying across the pale chest, untouched by sun, it looked not like the wound of a hero but an unsavoury thing, the sign of the body's failing, better hidden. Pearly shivered inwardly. There was that about him hinting of rottenness, decay – death? She wanted now to be away from him, from the foul breath, the large, shining nose, the eyes and the soft little paunch which bumped against her when they danced. She wanted to be in her safe, dull prison with its illuminations of another life beyond the cheap curtains.

"Maybe I'll see you there," she said, and ignored his outstretched hand. She did not want contact; she had noted that one of his fingers had an unhealed whitlow, raw, the swelling still evident. Another sign of the body's condition: a waning of the power to heal. She must get back to her room – quickly, quickly.

Pearl slipped out of the bar, lithe as a girl, before Noralf (with his heart) could get up and stop her. *Goodnight Juan, to the barman, goodnight Carlos on Reception, goodnight poor, sickly Noralf.*

Here was the lift, and Pearl stepped thankfully into the anonymous space, leaned against the grubby, blank walls as it slid upwards, jolting at every floor, exhaled long and hard, ridding herself of stale air and of Noralf. To kiss him! Unimaginable.

In the apartment, Pearl laughed at herself. The mirror showed her an ordinary face, glowing from sun and exercise, bare brown shoulders and a body that really she should not condemn just yet, not yet... there was a little time left, after all. *But not for the likes of you, Noralf, not for the likes of you!* She took a few floating steps to the Viennese waltz that sounded from the bar, and the hackneyed tune now struck her differently, seemed to hold some of the original nineteenth-century gaiety so lacking in the shabby room below.

Alone, Pearl starred in her own silver and blue ballet, twirling and circling, allowing her dress to riffle round her as the mirror caught the echoing flashes of her bracelet and earrings. She was graceful, serene, rising easily above the physical reality of this third-rate place and into somewhere that might be called happiness.

Out of breath, she stopped. A reek of stale sweat rose

from her clothes; but it was not hers, not her body's odour. She knew that intimately, could have identified it blindfold. She liked the tang of her own effluences – they were healthy, a sign of her organs doing their proper work. But this was the taint of another, not fresh, normal perspiration but rising out of something sinister, already moribund. Pearl shuddered violently. Nausea overwhelmed her.

Leaving her clothes in a hurried pile on the floor, Pearl jumped into the shower, turned the faucet on so hard that the water hit her fierce and sudden in the face, but she did not care. She wanted to drive out all the stink of that pathetic little man, to cleanse herself of the shoddiness of the bar, of what her life had become.

You're so lucky, they wrote to her from England. *Fancy, living and working in Spain!* Hollow echoes of imagined Costa glamour reached Pearl as she read these letters from envious sisters, friends. *I bet you meet lots of gorgeous men! Wish I was there.*

Pearl grimaced as she scrubbed, scrubbed away that smell, the taint of the reality of her life here that she did not ever write about and of which, when she returned to England for the summer holiday, fit and relaxed, she had no reason to speak. It took a long time, much longer than usual, before she was satisfied that it had all, quite gone. Purified, Pearl was now exhausted. She sat by her one-bar electric fire in the cool of the apartment as the winter wind blew from the mountains and sang her its weird, moaning tune. The music downstairs had stopped; a few heavy doors slammed, perfunctory goodnights were being said.

"Night, Alice. Night, Jim."

"Night, you two. See you tomorrow, Bob. Same time, same place?"

"Yeah. Where else is there?"

And laughter, slightly weary, cynical. Where else indeed?

The wind came stronger, colder. Pearl wrapped her bathrobe tightly round herself and prepared her mind for sleep.

* * *

Two days later she saw Noralf. She had not intended to go to the pool as she had promised, and she did not, but he caught her half way up the hill to the apartments. He regarded her reproachfully but humorously, his mild hound-eyes quite kind.

"You do not come today," he said.

Pearl looked at him. Reflected that she had, indeed, been rather cruel. He was asking if she would walk with him.

"Just around the garten. Then we can have coffee. Yes?"

In the sunlight, in the context of those pleasant gardens, with the backdrop of the purplish mountains, somehow reassuring in their majestic outline, he did not look so bad. Gauche, rather clumsy, ill dressed; but fresher, younger than she had remembered.

He smiled at her again, waiting.

The later afternoon sun struck pinkish-gold on the tops of the palm trees and the sweet spring air, like fine wine to the nose, drifted across, bringing the scent of wild flowers in its wake. Really, her life here was not so awful, Pearl thought. What was all that nonsense about decay and death?

"Well, all right," she said.

SOMETHING DIFFERENT

Rabat, 1988

RABAT WAS BEAUTIFUL. She could see that at once.

The anonymous, third-world squalor of Tangiers, almot two hundred miles by rail behind her, receded. Now, at the station entrance, the elegant boulevards of the Ville Nouvelle welcomed her with their measured tranqullity, that sense of old-world orderliness absent in contemporary European cities with their junketed mix of the clinically modern, the nondescript period pieces, the salvaged buildings of architectural grandeur, and everything in between. Here, a sort of early twentieth-century, almost colonial langour hung in the faintly moist air.

Travel-tired, confused, Harriet stood for a moment, pallid northern tourist on the threshhold of this darker, more brillliant place. Where was the Hotel Bon Accord? She peered hopelessly at the small, cramped map in the guide. A couple passed, speaking French; not the earthier, second-language dialect of Morocco, but the altogether sharper, faster sound of Paris. The girl, her short blonde hair cut in an indefinable, radical chic, the boy sallow, dark and intense.

"Excuse me."

She spoke in English, unable to drum up another tongue. The journey by land and sea, and then land again (the train) still jolted through her senses and in her nostrils lingered the close stink of the Tangiers port terminal toilets; straddling the slippery floor after a queasy ferry crossing, she had almost vomited and had got out as quic-

119

ly as possible to breathe in the fine dust and sunshine of a North African morning.

The couple turned, surprised out of their conspiratorial huddle.

"Do you know the way to the Hotel Bon Accord?"

The blonde head nodded; a brusque, authoritative movement.

"Yes, of course. It is quite near. We will take you."

"That's very kind of you – there's no need – I can find it if you direct me."

The French girl's cool, light eyes scanned Harriet unhurriedly. The boy looked at his feet.

"No problem. We are walking that way."

The tone – in near perfect, barely accented English – translated everything into the imperative: you simply did not argue with her.

It was a short distance after all. Harriet could have found it easily had she not been so tired, so extraordinarily weary, if her head and limbs had not been peculiarly heavy, almost to the point of inertness preventing motion.

Sluggishly, her tongue thickened by exhaustion and thirst, Harriet responded to their polite enquiries: the slightly aloof, correct social intercourse of the Parisian. She was here on holiday yes; touring, yes. No, she had not been to Morocco before, it was her first visit.

Bored by stilted trivialities, the girl lapsed into fast, colloquial French with her companion, many of the expressions new to Harriet's schoolgirl recollection. The language had moved on, without her. The large, wooden portals of Bon Accord stood open. It was early; only five o'clock in the afternoon, but already Harriet longed for sleep, her protesting body, which, dragged along for days, rebelling against the mind that had somehow detached itself, was now declaring that it needed a bed, any bed, the chance to restore itself and regain unity by a endless dive into hours – many hours – of unconsciousness.

Slowly, with a maddening lack of urgency, the concierge came forward from her sitting room. Her regard of the English woman was similarly impassive.

"Oui?"

Swiftly, the French girl stated the need for a room for – she indicated Harriet. Terms were quoted, negotiations carried out. A bath? A private WC? For one person, that was?

"Madame est suele?"

"Ou. Je suis seule. Et je preferais ensuite."

The flagging brain flickered onto automatic pilot, onto the last reserve of energy, just suficient to produce an involuntary response in French.

The girl's firm, wilful mouth dropped slightly open, and with disconcerted eyes she glanced at the boy, who stared intently at Harriet. They suddenly looked like startled deer, very young, their slick haircuts set strangely above their, naked, vulnerable faces. What had they been talking about on the way here? Harriet had been tired to listen, too preoccupied with basic needs to care.

Rapidly now, anxious to leave, the couple made thir farewells, scampered away on little clattering hooves, shaken out of their cool young confidence. Harriet shrugged. A sample of the so-called mystery of Morocco? It was not her concern.

The room was large, old, baroque: long drapes of burgundy procade, stuffed horsehair armchairs, a vast bed that was surely hard as brick, with a colourful woven cover. A washbasin, a shower, a screen. One or two native rugs. A little way down the corridor, a flush toilet which didn't smell, which apparently was for her sole use. Near this, on the flecked, marble floor, a dead cockroach in a swill of disinfectant. But the place was clean and the sheets fresh and sweet.

"It is all right, Madame?"

The young house porter looked at Harriet in appeal, hovered with her two light travelling bags. He was about twenty seven, or so, she estimated, tall, slim, with closely curling, wiry hair, so possibly part African Berber, and a small trimmed moustache. Attractive! flashed a momentary tagline in the gathering darkness inside Harriet's head.

"Yes, it's fine."

Remembered. Say more. One has to be fulsome here.

"It's a lovely room. I like it very much"

Oh for goodness; sake, any room will do. Just put down the cases so that I can throw myself onto that wonderful mirage of a bed, even if it is made of bricks, and sleep myself back to sanity. Tomorrow, and only tomorrow, I will wash.

And now he smiled, pleased, telling her about hot water and the times when she could get breakfast across the road.

"My friend's cafe – it is very French. Croissants and coffee and freshly squeeezed orange juice. Very good, most cheap."

"Yes, I see. That's great. You're very kind."

Go away, go away.

But he stood there. Something forgotten. The mental function rapidly closing idown into itself, hard to draw out what was needed. Remembered again. The tip. A few dirum.

"Here, for you. Thank you very much."

Go, please, please go.

"Bonsoir, Madame. I hope you sleep well."

"Thank you. Merci beaucoup. Bonsoir."

Oh God. Oh, thank God, the bed. Tear off shoes, rive at loose cotton trousers, sleep in tee-shirt and underwear, dropping things onto floor, anywhere, and the cockroaches, good luck to them, draw heavy curtains to shut out the softening evening light; oh hell yes, don't foget, most important: lock the door. Large, old-fashioned, hand-crafted key, rough flaking iron under the fingers, turn and lock, check the handle, yes, it's locked. And now the bed, it is concrete, but it doesn't matter, bunch up the stiff old French style pillow, curl in the head and sleep – here it comes! Down the long, spiralling web of exhaustion, weaving in and out the twists of confused and stumbling thought, tumult of waves of ebbing consciousness crashing over the aching head into the brain anaesthetising all feeling all sense and tide of blackness ringing darkness fading fading off and sleep …

* * *

Downstairs, in the high cool marbled hallway, Yassar took his place behind the idle reception desk. There was not much business this week. Madame La Concierge had paddled back to her private quarters, the hotel and the streets outside were empty. Rabat is so hushed; that's what strikes the traveller most forcibly. In all of crowded, noisy, colourful Morocco, this is almost a place without people, where only a few shadowy, cloaked figures haunt the wide, still streets. Even in the murmuring souks, the Medina, which Yassar knew much more intimately than the Ville Nouvelle, this holds true. By edict of the King, Rabat keeps itself quiet.

He stood and waited, passive as a munching beast, for the time to pass so that it would be possible for him to go off duty and slip down the broad, formal boulevard and into the warm light and the mingled, spiced smells of the evening souqs of the Medina. Here he might catch a late glass of tea with a friend, a stallholder in the market, as they finished business for the night, and then down the narrow network of alleys that reeked of generations of human occupation and through the dark, concealing doorway to his home. There was a small sleeping area for him in the hotel, of course, and Yassar did not go home every night; but when he was not required early the next day, or when his day off came round, then he returned to his own quarter of the city.

Yassar thought of his wife. She was pregnant again, very much so, and sickly, moody with it. Too often for his liking she turned him away these days.

"I am not well," she would say, and clamp her solid thighs together. "Leave me."

And she would close up her mouth against Yassar's seeking muzzle, and roll over in the lumpy bed.

Or their other child, a boy of nearly two, would cry out, and Bushra would say,

"Oh, go to him, Yassar. I must sleep."

It seemed to him that all women wanted was to sleep. Madme La Concierge, now, she dozed and snored in her back sitting room and the bell had to ring long and impatiently before she heard it. Bushra slept a lot these days and she too snorted and grunted as she runtled round the mattress. Sometimes Yassar wondered if she was the same woman he had married, or whether some malicious Djinn had not come in the night and changed the slender, loving bride who had clung to him so appealingly into this fattened, unpredictable creature on whose sagging breast one child hung and in whose swelling, hard belly another was fast growing.

And then there was the English woman. She was much

older than his wife, Yassar judged, as much as forty maybe, but remained attractive in the way that these western women seemed to manage. Blondeish gold hair, reddened pale skin with freckles that Yssar found particularly intriguing, blue eyes very clear even though they were undershadowed with weariness. Good breasts, he had noted, their firm fullness evident under the light, sweat-stained top she wore; rounded hips and well shaped ankles. He wondered if she had borne children; her body did not display the usual, unsightly signs, but you could never tell.

"Ah yes," thought Yassar, absently paring his nails, "I could let my ideas wander with you if I wanted."

But she too, all she wanted to do was sleep. And before six o'clock in the afternoon! It was clear from the way she had dismissed him. Not that Yassar would have dreamed of approaching her; La Concierge would throw him out, and kill him, or kill him first and then throw his remains to the ants. But the English woman had not even looked at him, her dullling eyes turning to the unyielding bed only in longing for sleep.

"What is it with these females?" Yassar turned his eyes up to the peeling paintwork of the ceiling, as if reading an answer from the deity there. "All-powerful Allah, did you really make their brains so feeble as to require this continual torpor?"

Yassar himself, he worked ten or twelve hours a day at the hotel, after which he would go for a tea and an idle chat with his friend in the souq, and only then go home to his own house, where he wanted most urgently to make love to his wife and talk with her for a while. Sometimes he would take the road out of the Medina, uphill to the white walls of the Casbah, and down again to the sea where the road followed the beach to the river estuary, with Sale on the other side. There he would stare at the dark, foaming Atlantic and feel the light, night wind whipping his skin, and gaze upward at the brilliant myriad stars. Onece, he had had a girl on the beach. That was when Brushra was pregant the first time, but he was ashamed afterwards and regetted it. The girl was foreign, a traveller sleeping rough; and she had laughed at him, calling him things in a tongue he did not understand.

The huge plain face of the hotel clock inched its hands round until the hour when La Concierge would waddle through.

"You might as well go now," she would say, lookng at the clock over the half-rimmed glasses as if she suspected it of conspiring to deceive her. "It is after ten, and I will lock up for tonight."

"Goodnight, Madame."

"Goodnight, Yassar. Do not be late for your next duty."

"I am never late, Madame."

"Hm. And you never tell lies either. Go home."

And up yours, Mdame La Concierge, thinks Yassar on such occasions as he gladly deserts his post.

In the dark, hushed room, two floors above, Harriet slept. Oblivion had come rushing in at once, swift as a bird covering her face with its thick, soft wings. For three, four, five hours she slept thus, moving hardly at all, her body stiffening on the bullet-hard mattress, a discomfort that in the morning would be pain. Deeper she sank, shedding the weariness of three days of non-stop travel as a swimmer rids herself of the last hampering garments, to float naked and free in reviving, cool waters. Three days of flight she had taken, three days of heading fast, fast to this holiday.

"Something different," her friends had promised her. "You'll adore Morocco, it really is different."

Three days of traversing a lateral to get away from what she knew too well; three days of overland journeying, not allowing herself the luxury of literal flight by air; and now, having reached some unspecified, indeterminate point, she could permit, indeed could no longer hold off, the long, plunging descent into the unconscious in order to reclaim the self that was so nearly lost in all that precipitate running. Or which, perhaps, had been lost, unheeded, some time before.

* * *

Outside, Yassar checked the heavy doors, secured the outer grille, and walked to the tranquil Medina. Amer welcomed him with fresh mint tea, and they talked of the prices of things and the gossip of the native quarter.

"I see Ghazi has got himself a new stall, then. He's got some fancy stuff there."

"Well, that's true – but he'd better run it better than the last one. Such prices!"

"He was looking for the tourists. Thought he'd make it rich with the Americans."

"Huh! They don't by much in the souqs, and when they do they bargain you into the ground, expecting something for nothing. Why, only last week I asked thirty dirums for something and the Yank, he said – wait for it! – five. FIVE! Of course, we met half way, but still."

"It's a hard life."

The two men sighed, and gave themselves more steaming tea from the small brass heating stove. Minty vapour rose into the chilling, clammy air. It was early April, and the nights could still be cold.

Yassar stood, stretched his long arms.

"I must go to my wife."

His friend looked at him sympathetically.

"She's pregnant again, I hear."

"Yes."

Yassar sighed again. He paused. His eyes grew large, moist, brilliant, with the inner light of the instinctive actor. The tall, sinewy body struck a pose.

"And I am suffering with it – how I am suffering!"

And both men doubled up in laughter, mocking Yassar, mocking themselves, cocking a snook at life.

Amer clapped his friend on the shoulder, and they embraced.

"See you tomorrow, incha'allah!"

Slowly, Yassar wandered beyond the squared confines of the Medina. Tonight he did not feel like going straight back to his snoring, swollen wife, and so he took the customary, solitary walk to the beach. Certainly, it was a little risky to stay out late and alone, but Yassar did not care. A restlessness fell upon him, something he could not pin down or define. He felt like doing somersaults, handsprings, walking hundreds of miles, climbing mountains, dancing, singing; but the one thing for sure he did not feel like was sleeping.

Next to the estuary he found a flat, wide rock, and sat motionless for a while, staring into the darkness in front and above him with straining eyes, his head pushing forward as if in this way he would pull something out of that black space that would answer his need. The lights of Sale began to go out; the dark hours passed. There was no moon, only a misty starlight, and the night was wintry. Yassar wrapped his thin jacket round him and wished he had called by home for his djellaba.

With his hands he trailed a little sand either side of the rock, running the thin dry stuff mechanically through and through his fingers as his head sank slowly upon his knees; a heavy mist was settling over the city, a dampness in the air. The King would be going south to Marrakech if the weather stayed like this, and then the city would be emptier than ever as the faithful poured out to follow him. Yassar had never seen the place. He had been been once or twice to Tangiers, though it had not impressed him except with its general vileness. But they said Marrakech was nice.

"It's a red city," they would tell him. "Marrakech blushes at her own beauty!"

All would laugh at the well-worn joke, but Yassar would only pout, preparing for complaint.

"Fat chance I have of seeing Marrakech. We can only just live on what I earn from the hotel – that mean old bitch."

"You don't do so badly. You should stop getting your wife pregnant, that's what."

"Tell me how."

"You know very well how! Do you need us to inform you?"

And the men would slap each other and roll about again. All knew how impossible it was to subdue that youthful, irrepressible, neverending male desire that rose again and again like the phoenix from the ashes of its own quick satisfaction.

At last, after many drifting hours, as a chill light wind blew up, Yassar felt his eyes grow sluggish. The restlessness subsided a little, layers of sleep running in on top of it as the crested waves slapped over each other onto the beach, wetting the silvered, smooth sand. Soon the layers were a floor, a sea, and ocean, and Yassar's neat, dark head dropped under it, flopped between his parted legs, his hands fell slackly onto the rocks, and he slept.

It was three in the morning, and the twin cities of Rabat and Sale were hushed as a drugged infant, wrapped in their swirling coat of low cloud which shut out the bright heavens. The muezzins were stilled, awaiting their four-thirty call, and even the barking dogs succumbed, sensing the magic of those empty hours when nothing, and anything, happens.

* * *

In her thickly-curtained room, Harriet lay unmoving as a corpse, flat on her back, breathing deeply, unaccustomedly loudly, on the rigid bed. She had slept now for several hours and still her body said it needed more. In all these hours she had dreamed little, her mind shutting down even on that release. Dreams demand energy, said her brain, and that I haven't got.

And so Harriet's sleep was of the kind where one can recall afterwards only shutting one's eyes, a split second of profound inky blackness and then the awakening to the hospital recovery room, or a brilliant morning.

Suddenly –

The beclothes were pulled crudely back. A panting. A man's hoarse, panting breath. On her. One top of her. He was on top of her, this slim young form, this young man. Outlined against the darkness of the opened door she could make out even in the fog of her sleep the tightly curled head, the face of the hotel porter in stark profile. Quickly he pushed aside the remainng obstacles: the sheet, her tee-shirt, pants, his own light garments, and then he was in her with one massive, imperious thrust, his body weightless and undemanding, all his power focussed on that distended organ, rudely opening her legs and thrusting bluntly once, twice, three times, the shock of it forcing her head back against the stiff pillow. His eyes gleamed in the half-light with a sort of anguisehed excitement.

130

She heard him groan something: an endearment, perhaps, an expression of pleasure? But no, this sounded threatening, this guttural Arabic, the very language a sort of violence in the throat.

"Okay, English lady Now I'll take you!"

Once -

"Oh yes, I'll have you all right. Stupid stuck up English bitch!"

Twice –

"Don't struggle, lady. I could just kill you if you do."

Thrice – the ruthless, mechanistic pumping an accompaniment to the harshness of the strange spitting, choking utterances which she did not comprehend but by terror translated into menace of the blackest, most malevolent kind.

"Please! Oh, please, stop!"

Harriet fought to raise herself; he was not lying weightily upon her, in fact the only physical contact she could feel was that part of him that was so overwhelmingly in her, as if the rest of him were somehow floating slightly above, and as she did so cried out. Her heart pounded unpleasantly, booming in her chest in great, uneven leaps, and her tongue constricted after the first raw, compulsive cry. She was being raped! They'd told her about this too, warned her that it could happen in Morocco, that a western woman travelling alone should take great care, but she had dismissed this as exaggeration, shameful racism, prejudice of the meanest kind.

The form above her seemed not to hear, his head raised staring wild-eyed into the darkness as if in some strange trance, every muscle concentrated on the slow, deliberate driving movement. Harriet gathered her small remaining strength.

"Get out! Leave me! I will call the police!"

The light figure paused, the head turned as though listening to something.

"Go away! I will scream very loudly and they will catch you. Stupid boy. Everyone knows who you are!"

Suddenly –

He was gone. He was not there. There was no sign of anyone, no man was in her room. Harriet sat up, easily; consciousness and its companion of wakeful fear erupted over her. The bedclothes were orderly, her garments in place. No shaft of light came in through the closed bedroom door. The room was absolutely silent.

After a moment, Harriet slid from the bed and went to the door. Locked. The key, still on the inside, firmly in the locked position. She shook it, disbelieving. Nobody could have got in here – unless – unless It was possible that the lock was flimsy, that it could be opened from the outisde, bypushing, andd then be pulled shut again. She tried an experimental tug. Harder. The door, solid and imposing, did not move. Nothing in the bed was disturbed; there was no telltale wetness between her legs.

It had seemed so real. Harriet leaned against the dusty, dry wood of the door for a moment, feeling yet that aching, deserate force that was so alarming but also had echoes of the strangest, purest, most overpowering form of pleasure. Had her spontaneous cry been one of warning, or of ecstasy?

But her heart still beat high in her chest, and fright was uppermost. It had been a dream, that was clear, but such a dream! Was this what exhaustion did to you? Was this what happened when you pushed yourself to the extreme? Perhaps in the free-floating state of limbo, ultimate letting-go, things drifted up from the unconscious that were better left there.

Yes, said Harriet's bright sharp intellect with its guardi-

132

an eye switched on, that would be it. That explains it. Just an aberration of the conscious mind, quite common in cases of extreme fatigue.

Yes, that explained it. Nothing had in fact happened at all. Relaly, it was very ordinary; Freudian even, mundane. A sexual fantasy dream! At her age. She put a hand to her unsteady bosom and smiled ruefully to herself in the dark.

"Nothing happened," she murmured to herself, and unthinkingly repated the soothing words that long, long ago her mother had used to settle a child. "Nothing to worry about, nothing at all."

Something in Harriet's inner body, the fleshly self never seen or apprehended, that functioned quietly, obediently, undetected all those years – something here stirred faintly in protest; but the watchful intellect frowned sternly, and the little flutter subsided.

"Nothing happened," she repeated, like a mantra. "Just a dream."

Gradually the heartbeat slowed, the quietness of the room ironing smooth her tumbled thoughts, until she could return to the calm, unruffled bed and sleep again.

* * *

Yassar chuntered and shifted restlessly on his hard rock bed under the murky night sky. It was very cold and damp now, but he did not feel it. The strain of keeping himself awake on the high peak of his own nervous energy had driven him into profound, insensible sleep. He felt nothing, was aware of nothing, knew and dreamed nothing.

Suddenly – he was in a hotel room, in pitch blackness, the weak locked door opening readily under his slight shove. Panting with excitement and desire, he was gliding silently to a bed on which a lady lay in torpid slumber.

Roughtly, impatiently, he wrenched at the bedclothes, her clothes, his own flimsy garments, put his urgent hand between her soft, white thighs and swiftly drove the rod of his burgeoning need into her slack, receptive body. Moaning with gratitude and love, for yes, he loved this marvellous, fair-skinned lady, he continued with his pleasure, which surely must bring joy to her, so great was it, so deeply, deeply satisfying.

"Beloved!" he cried, in his own language.

Once -

"I love you, I desire you. Let me take you, beloved."

Twice –

"Beautiful Khamar, lady of the moon, be my love."

Three times did the marvellous, giving member put joy into the lady, three times Yassar gave her of himself. He was nearing the very summit of his longing.

But then! She shrieked, sat up like the waking dead, screamed terrible things at him like a witch, her opaque eyes glittering in the thin stream of light from the doorway, cursing him, raining evil wishes on him and ranting like a mad woman.

"You will be eaten alive!" he heard. And then, "You will be thrown to the rats, cut into small pieces for the vermin to feed on."

And next she cursed him with the venom of a scorpion.

"Your loins will be poisoned! Your issue will be damned!"

Fear flooded Yassar's genitals, the wam fluids running cold. Swiftly he moved his poised body off her, pulled up his thin trousers and sped away, into the mists of the night, through locked doors and iron grilles, his form winging back to himself, back to the tired, miserable Yassar on the beach by the churning Atlantic, where cognisance came, unwelcome with the first chill morning light.

He sat up stiffly, his strong heart beating uncomfortably and painfully in his chest. His knees were rheumatic from the unnatural posture in which he had fallen asllepp. He stared around him in the thinning darkness, felt the trickling sand under his fingers, heard the soft shushing of the sea a few metres away. Where was the English woman, the moon-lady? Where was he? Had he not possessed her? No, how could that be possible? For here he was, sitting cold as the mountain snows at Imlil, on the beach below the Casbah, shivering like a man who has caught pneumonia.

It had been a dream, that was all.

"Yes, I had a dream,"muttered Yassar to himself. "Most definitely, that is what it was."

Ahah, said Yassar's cooperative conscience, yes, you had a sort of nightmare. That's all. You saw this English lady, your wife is – well, as she is just now, and that was enough Any man could have this thing happen to him.

That explained it.

"Nothing happened," Yassar repeated. "Nothing at all," he said to his dazed self. What unkind tricks the mind could play, eh?

For a moment, he leaned back against the jutting rock. The hard points stuck in his back like vicious reminders of reality, jabbing him into full awareness. It was painful, but reassuring. Here was rock, here was sand, sea, here was Yassar. Not in any lady's bedroom, nor in her bed. Just a silly, adolescent dream! And he a father, a husband, and soon to be made a father agin. That was his life, his everyday, known life.

But something embedded in Yassar's lately disturbed loins rose again, pre-erection even, protested very weakly; the memory stirred the chill flesh and set a spark. And then it died. Yassar leaned back hard, deliberately, against the obdurate stone, which pricked him with the malice of a demon. Foolish, stupid Yassar.

Dragging himself painfully to his feet, Yassar shook his head and stumbled down to the sea to sluice his face in the abrasive salt water. There he stood for a moment, staring dully into the lightening dawn sky over the city of Rabat. Soon the muezzins would begin to wail. He had better get home before that. He checked his garments. Yes, they were all in order, only a little dampened and creased from his night on the beach.

Now he could sympathise with the women's desire to sleep. That was all he wanted to do. He had a day off, that was lucky. With jerky steps he trudged up the path to the Casbah, walked round it and onto the main city road, over the hill and down into the Medina, into his own alley and his own house where his wife lay noisily sleeping. She stirred briefly at his entry and grumbled.

"And where to you think you've been, uh? With some girl, I shouldn't wonder."

If only you knew! thought Yassar. Aloud, he replied ill humouredly.

"Mind your own business."

"Am I to be left alone at night, every night?" she demanded, plucking at the covers.

"Be quite, woman. I'm tired enough, without you going on at me. Go to sleep. You're always asleep so get back to it."

Yassar slipped off his few clothes and slid into bed beside her, and fell at once into the labyrinth of darkness which offers reprieve without reproof.

One brief, flashing last thought swam in front of his eyes.

"The English woman will go today. I shall not see her again."

But whether he was glad or sorry, Yassar was too tired to tell.

* * *

On the following duty day, the Thursday of that week as it turned out, Yassar was startled to see the English woman at the reception desk early in the morning.

She appeared calm, rested, looking pretty and refreshed in her fine, pale blue shirt with the sleeves rolled up and her soft, patterned cotton skirt, worn discreeetly long for islam. Briskly, she settled up her bill with Madame la Conceierge, more confident in her somewhat old-fashioned French now that she had slept two good nights.

Yassar took his place by the door, his face as expressionless as it was possible for him to make it. What an idiot he was! As if she would even take a second glance at him, this rather beautiful, older European lady.

"Thank you, Yassar," she said, as he opened the front grille for her. "You see, I did like my room, very much. And so I stayed another day."

"I am happy," murmured Yassar. He did not dare to look directly at her. It was clear to him from this woman's breezy manner that she had never looked at him as a man. His ridiculous dream now seemed even more outlandish and risible. His finger gripped the iron of the gate, turning the strong brown skin white over the knuckles, willing her to go, willing her to stay.

"Well, goodbye, Madame."

The English woman paused on the doorstep, perhaps searching for the right words in French.

"I shall come back to Rabat some time – and I shall stay here again."

But she spoke to the concierge, not to him. Yassar turned away.

"Au revoir, Madame. You will always be welcome."

And La Concierge allowed herself a tight smile, removed the stern, schoolteacher half glasses, and smiled agiain, a little more widely. Yassar was amazed. This was almost unknown, this camerarderie with guests. What mysterious charms did this Englishwoman cast?

"Yes." Harriet hestitated, fumbling in the language she had to strive to remember. "My friends told me that if I wanted a holiday that was unusual, I should come to Morocco, that I would find – "

Again, the hestiation. And then, very deliberately, it seemed to Yassar,

"– something different."

Later, in the clean, quiet, air-conditioned Class I rail carriage, Harriet allowed herself to reflect. The departure, seeing Yassar standing silent and indifferent by the door, had been difficult, and she had had to put herself on that automatic pilot again, to sweep past him without a pause or a weakening of the spirit, a giving-in to impulse. Such inclincations in a woman of the world such as she!

But he had not looked at her at all, indeed, he had rattled the door in some irritation, probably impatient for her to be on her way; she need not have been concerned. Understandably, he did not see her a a woman. Why should he? She was forty-one, inclined to a slight plumpness and with a freckled complexion; quite an old hag to him. No doubt he had some luscious girl somewhere in the old town who kept him busy.

That ludicrous dream! How could she have? Amused at her manifest transparency (to have subliminal yearnings about a Moroccan houseboy! How he would make a joke of it with his friends if he were to know!) Harriet smiled

138

at her reflection as the train cruised effortlessly, silently along the long, curving rail to Marrakech, saw in the thick double-glazed panel the gentle, English face and blushed, deeply, at her own long-forgotten beauty.

THE STATION MASTER'S WIFE

He was showing off again, of course; this time in a different language; consequently, she was excluded as so often these days. The broad back of her husband, with just the beginnings of an old man's hunch, was turned in a sixty-five degree angle so that the station-master's wife was obliged to peep like a feebly rising moon over his shoulder.

Bored, perhaps, by the shopping trip to Port Said, he had found compensation – or was it revenge? – in talking to this Frenchwoman, responding as all men are wont to do to the absurd fluttering of helpless, slim white hands.

"I can't make them understand!" she had cried, in her pretty accent. "I speak no Arabic, you see, and they don't – they don't –"

Rouafa's husband leaned across and took the piece of paper that the extravagantly soft little hands clutched.

"Ah," he said, in passable French. "They have issued this from the Tourist Information Office, yes?"

"Why, you speak my language!" The woman clapped her hands smartly, like a seal. "And so well, too."

The crescent of Rouafa's countenance slid back into the dense cloud of her abaya, until only a shadowy sliver could be seen. The bird's beak lines that soured a mouth once piquante, captivating even, deepened and drooped.

"This ticket," he continued, twitching the shoulder over which his wife waxed and waned, "this ticket is for the second class carriage without air conditioning. You are sitting in the air-conditioned section."

Delicate hands flew to the delicate mouth, which did

not droop but lay in a neat, slightly curving line that lent wistfulness to the flawless face.

"Oh dear. So I have to move – back there?"

The Frenchwoman pointed through the intersecting door. Every time it was opened, a marked odour of stale urine from the adjoining lavatory drifted through their compartment. Hakim shifted in his seat, wrestling with the expanding buttocks of his wife, who as usual was pressed far too close to him. This was her habit, and it irritated him, as so much about her did. He would have liked to blot her out completely, eclipse her, squash her so tightly against the side of the carriage that she would ooze like a dark stain out into the night and leave him alone. But of course he could not; how would it look in the eyes of this elegant French lady? Distinctly uncivilised, and France, he knew, was a most cultured place; one had only to speak the language, as he did, to be aware of it.

"Look," he said, patting one of the agitated wrists, "don't worry. You can stay in this compartment until we get off. I'm station master at Zougzag, so nobody will argue with it. Then just for the rest of the journey, to Tanta, which is not so far, you can sit through there."

The Frenchwoman quivered, outwards as it were from her small, dainty nose to the extremities of fingers and feet.

"It's not that bad," said Hakim encouragingly, as to a child. "We're going over half way. And there's always a couple of policemen on the train. You'll be quite safe."

The woman's hands composed themselves, came to rest like calmed birds.

"You're very kind."

"What was all that about?"

And now here were the sharp claws of his wife bedding themselves into the mercifully padded back of his jacket. The rough, colloquial sounds of his own tongue struck him harshly like a *sirocco* about the ears. Such a woman! How could she ever have excited him, in the early days of their marriage, with those horny nails?

Oh, she was given the wrong sort of ticket at Tourist Information, he said, hardly bothering to turn his head, so that he had to slide his eyes sideways towards his wife in order to preserve at least the appearance of marital courtesies.

"She has a problem?" Rouafa's sullen face lifted, its discontent shifting subtly to a vicarious enthusiasm. "Well, if she has a problem, let her come and sleep at our house." And to his further horror, she indicated to the French lady the pantomime of sleep, two hands folded child-like under the cheek, the sagging eyes squeezed tightly shut.

Hakim wriggled in discomfort. So often now she embarrassed him: with her fatness, the pain she got in her legs and which she demonstrated to the world by contortions of expression and slow, exaggerated rubbing of the knees, and by an awkward, hobbling walk whenever she could remember. If this was the face of martyrdom, Hakim reflected, thinking of his wife's purposeful, twisted agonies, it would do badly for the cause.

"Don't be so stupid!" he hissed at her out of the corner of his mouth, forgetting that the Frenchwoman would not understand.

"What does your wife say?"

Drat it. Drat everything: fat wives, shopping excursions for yet more un-needed quality bed linens and towels which apparently could only be found in Said, and this damnably slow, stopping train on which they conveniently got free seats because of his position on the railways; to hell with everything. He could see that his wife was going to get in on it, that if he wasn't careful he would end up as a mere go-between, an intermediary, whilst these women exchanged remarks about nothing, as women always did.

"Ah," he said, casually furious. "My wife says that if you are worried you can stay with us, at our house in Zougzag, for the night."

The words came out like lumps of stale bread, reluctantly coughed up; but what else could he do or say in these dreadful circumstances? The whole thing was becoming an unbearable strain; to prolong it until tomorrow was not even thinkable. But he need not trouble himself; she would not accept. This refined, expensively dressed lady, would not want to stay at the house of some unknown locals. Though their home, well, he could be proud of what he had been able to provide. It had covers on all the couches and the walls were painted, not just concrete or shoddy plaster like so many, and the patches of damp were regularly scraped off and washed over, treated, not left to go black and fungal as in so many places he saw. And he had to admit that Rouafa, with her old chicken's face and her rheumatic knees, kept their house as a man likes to find it; she had also put in some feminine touches that he did not begrudge, for they warmed the soul on a cold evening. Still, it would not do for this lady, whose own home, he knew, would be one of utmost luxury; and in any case, what can pass a pleasant hour or two on a tedious journey can become an intolerable awkwardness if prolonged. To have this woman in his house for the night, to have to sleep beside obese, sluggish Rouafa, lying awake himself in order not to let out his customary loud, vibrating night-time farts; to have to spring out of bed extra early tomorrow so as to wash and brush his hair and make his collar stand up clean and fresh; all this he did not relish at all, and his heart curdled sadly in his chest.

But the Frenchwoman had saved him, naturally, for she was genteel, not like this gauche creature who had mothered his three daughters and two sons.

"I would not put your wife to such trouble. She must be very tired after so long a day. And in any case, I am to be met at Tanta."

This was a lie; one is not met at Tanta unless one has family stretching generations back, or a sound business connection (in which case you would be a man and probably arriving in daytime hours), but it was a graceful, good lie, and he relaxed, smiling at her.

"What did she say?" nagged the moon-face of his wife. "Will she come?"

"No, of course not." The words shot like pellets from a catapult. "She is being met by friends, and in any case she has booked into a hotel."

This compounded lie fell easily from the tongue, but not so graciously as the Frenchwoman had managed it. Hakim was conscious of his beastliness, though he forgave himself at once. After all, his wife was these days but a disappointment to him. The faintly crooked eyes, with the downturned corner at one of them, were but distortions of the originals, and the surrounding flesh that dragged the face towards old age pulled the expression with it, leaving only an impression of malcontent. The chin, pertly pointed in youth, now had its companions which trembled whenever high feelings were aroused; thank God, this was not so often, for Rouafa was lazy in temperament, with the bovine placidity of the emotionally languid, prone more to silent pouting than to rage.

The Frenchwoman was making polite conversation, to cover the embarrassment of the previous few minutes and to temper the rejection. Had they children? And what were they all doing – quite grown up, she assumed? – all those things that are easy to answer, the automatic, well-practised responses soothing and smoothing the way.

"Yes, we have five."

Five? Oh, how glorious, how wonderful to have such a family. He must be very proud. Yes?

Yes, indeed, perhaps he should not be so unkind about his wife. She had given him his sons, his two longed-for boys; and then there were the girls – though strangely, the boys were disappointing, the older one a whimsy creature with the same sulky pout to the mouth as his mother, the other with that suspicion of a droop to one eye, and neither of them had excelled in school as he, Hakim, had done so many years ago. Really, though it was odd for a father to say it, he was prouder of his daughters – one at University, one working already in a government department, one young married to an ambitious thirty year old who had provided them with a flat in Cairo's new city. The second son, the youngest of the family, reminded Hakim at the birth of the last feeble bit of shit strained out of one's arse, an afterthought, a puny, wizened egg dropped by an exhausted mother eagle. He constantly had some slight sickness, some troubling little ailment, and Rouafa worried herself over the lad in a way that drove a man to exasperation and storming out of the house. Samir's progress at school was slow; he would be lucky if his father could get him low-paid a job on the railways at this rate. Such advantages the boy had, and all going to waste; whereas he, Hakim, had made his father boast of him.

But here were the women at it again, asking and answering questions through him as he thought of other things, though he should not blame the Frenchwoman, who was, of course, merely being courteous. How enchantingly she managed it, including his wife in the conversation, though clearly not out of predilection, and without making him feel in the least remorseful. Not that he should feel any

146

such chagrin: if his wife was too brainless and idle to learn another language, that was not his fault.

A silence followed, the routine questions having run out. There are only so many things you can ask without seeming prurient, and in any case, they had more or less reached the limits of Hakim's grasp of French. Small, low houses flashed by in the darkness, the single electric bulbs strung on wires from house to house lighting up their shabby, crumbling walls, the earth floors and glimpses of mean interiors. Outside, sometimes, the men had lit fires on the dirt paths, and sat on their haunches round the cheerful flames that warmed them in the moist, cool air and the mist that rose from the distant river and the marshland, so chilling after the heat of the day.

With satisfaction Hakim thought of his own, fine house in the station yard. He deplored these peasants, who washed their oxen along with themselves in the rivers, soiling the waters that everyone had to drink; and he shuddered momentarily at the thought of the French lady sitting amongst them in the cheaper carriage behind. It was a passing moment, but one in which he reflected that it might have been better had she accepted his wife's offer; but then, nothing like that happened in reality, and in any case she would survive. Brushing aside his concern as easily as he did his wife's imploring face, Hakim looked forward to home. He was tired. They would go their ways, and life would go on the same.

Now his wife was asking for a photograph of the Frenchwoman. Was there to be no end to his mortification? She was behaving like some coy teenager with a crush.

"I have not one of myself," his wife indicated by gestures, "but I want a picture of you." Impudently, she stabbed a finger in her husband's arm. "Tell the lady I would like her to write to me, and I will write to her."

"For God's sake." Hakim lost all patience. "You inane creature, how are you going to manage that? You cannot write a word of French, and this good lady knows no Arabic."

"Then you will translate," replied his wife with her indolent calm, lifting the lowered lid slightly so that he could see the gleam of a green eye. "Go on. Tell her. *Tell her.*"

The French lady was rooting in her bag, and had produced a passport picture of herself. Hakim noted that it was not flattering.

"Write on it," his wife gestured, and with a deprecatory laugh the woman did so: "Votre amie, Helene."

"There," she said, and passed the photograph across Hakim to Rouafa. "Now. Give me your address and I will write to you."

Hakim saw that she now spoke directly to his wife, but of course in French, so that he was obliged to interpret. This was the effect his boorish wife had on this gentlewoman! Rouafa nodded and smiled, lifting the corners of her mouth with a sudden, old-remembered charm; the green eye-slits glinted. Hakim, bypassed, knew himself redundant, even as an interloctuor; these women understood each other in the strange and unfathomable way that females did.

He knew that the Frenchwoman would not write; that the cheap snap would join the ranks of family snapshots on his wife's dresser for a while, that she would take it up and look at it for a week or two, and that it would fall behind the sideboard one day and be forgotten. He knew that the French woman knew all that too. As for Rouafa, she would not be thinking beyond tonight; and it did not matter. The purpose of the exercise had been accomplished. They had woven their net around him, these two, but he could see no point at which the clever, quick fibres of their minds, their damned evil feminine souls could have been stayed. It was a pattern that wove men out, left them to go down to the cafe and smoke a hookah and talk with other men also pushed from the succour of their women's lives.

But then, he knew that Rouafa was, after all, no fool. He might call her idiotic, might revile the sleepy, half-shut eyes, but she was sharp enough to know that he was disenchanted with her. She would also know that, despite this, he was faithful. Some unspoken bond between them said that marriage was a kind of routine, like a job that you stuck to for life. He would sleep beside her in the wide bed, empty now of the children, till death left one of them alone. He would turn to her out of need for many years ahead, as prompt each time as the trains that ran from Cairo to Port Said, grunting like an old engine and hissing as he shunted into his destination, on schedule, like the timetable in his own station. In fact, his wife would probably be able to work out the hour by him as the noise he made, and the screaming express, combined in the darkness to deafen the ears and blot out the world for those moments. Only theirs was a journey that did not often bring much pleasure to the travellers these days; Rouafa aware of her declining charm, Hakim conscious of the monotony of his own performance in the mundane safety of the bed that was their only point of conjugation. By day, he shifted himself increasingly from her, and she, likewise, shut her hooded eyes against him, the pains in her knees growing fiercer and her complaining ever more resonant.

Hakim felt his spirit descend into an abyss; he hated what the day had been, hated his round, cunning wife, detested the slyness of the French with their deceitful air of refinement that ensnared a man; hated Port Said, shopping, and this rattling, unheated train in the cold night. It would be good to return to work tomorrow, and visit the cafe in the evening, in the logic and sanity of a man's domain.

"Zougzag," announced his wife, rubbing the smeared window.

He looked at her, twisting his body through the angle of remove he had kept all the way; there was something in her voice that pulled him. She smiled: an eager smile, and her green eyes that went with her fair skin and lighter hair opened wide as she gazed out through the thick darkness to the points of light that meant the station, and their house. She sat upright; the pallid cheeks coloured. She looked younger, all at once, and Hakim sneaked a look at her, looked down surreptitiously at the photograph of the French woman, which made the lady look considerably older than he had thought her.

And then he knew; knew that Rouafa was happy to return to her home, happy to be married to the station master, that she was proud of him, despite the obligatory nature of their contact; and he knew that this flirting of his, and also of hers with the French woman, had been a mere diversion, a game; for him, a commonplace boosting of his male ego, but for Rouafa, something to amuse her intuitive, bright mind that she kept hidden behind the weighted lids, and also, when she chose, beneath her veil. He also knew that she had put him in his place, had outwitted him; and inwardly he laughed, the drollness of the situation warming a husbandly heart.

For she was his wife; of all these years, his loyal wife, cooking and keeping his house good and bearing his children; not her fault that they were mostly girls, and in any case, who cared: girls were as good as boys these days, at least his daughters were with their university degrees, their business skills and their sharp wits, like their parents'. She was his bride, this plump woman who had grown sleek on the fat of the land that he had provided, and he could be proud of her and of them both for being what they were.

Now she stood up, rubbing her painful legs with that rueful expression that he pitied, at the bottom of his obstinate nature, and so he helped her, gruffly, uttering words of sympathy and getting down the heavy bags, urging her into the aisle as one does a reluctant mule.

"Come," he said, murmuring the rolling Arabic of the region. "We'll soon be at home and in our nice, warm bed."

Rouafa looked at him obliquely out of the clear, olive eyes. She rubbed her knee, and then slid her hand slowly upwards on her thigh, as if in pain; only her face no longer contorted, but smiled at him as her hand, her well-fleshed hand with its long pointed nails moved up and down, up and down, and a little further up her heavy leg. Desire stabbed like a knife-blade, keen as ever, as sometimes happened even now. Hakim hurried his wife out of the train, rushing his goodbyes to the Frenchwoman who was, he noticed now, abominably thin. Rouafa hardly acknowledged her; there was no need. She had her photo, and now she could go home and fuel again the fire that she kept alight somehow, all through the years.

The train pulled slowly away, like a drifting beast, out of the mists of Zougzag station, and the Frenchwoman was left to move to the smells and the filth of the lower class carriage. There she had, after all, quite an amusing time with the chattering locals, and carelessly put down the scrap of paper on which the station master had unwillingly written the address. The scrap fell amongst other scraps, amongst crumbs and cigarette ends and the dust of a thousand feet, and at the next station stop it blew unheeded through the briefly opened door and back down the marshes, caught in their web of clouded air, and along the line that marks out this precious, thin green fertile strip, to swirl beyond the lights, the fires, the mean huddle of dwellings and into the empty desert that swallows everything without a sound, and where there are no questions and no answers, only silence.

THE TREASURE

ONE COULD SEE clearly that she was pregnant. The pink, nylon overall they gave her to wear stretched taut over the swelling bump; about five and a half months of bump, one would have estimated.

Summer was at its zenith. The bar was not fully air-conditioned, and the girl sweated, a little damp dark moustache of perspiration forming over her smooth mouth. She worked in a sort of endless circle of motion – chopping, sweeping, mopping, slicing, wiping and sweeping; but it all came back to the same point: cheap hired labour. Fourteen hours a day when the tourist season packed the bar Eva worked, barely lifting her head, her face concealed in the shadow of her short, bobbed shiny black hair.

But she was lucky, she had to remember this; most definitely lucky. She may have been cheap labour, but she was special. In this Catholic country she was carrying that most precious of burdens in her blessed womb: a child. The customers would eye her with admiration, respect. " So strong, such a marvellous little thing, to work so well with that growing weight," they would murmur, and the bar owners would smile on her fondly, proudly; they liked having this pregnancy in their place and besides, it reflected well on how good they were being to her. They shared her pregnancy, yes they did. They would asked her most solicitously each day how she felt.

"Are you well this morning? Did you sleep all right? And how is the little one in there?"

The girl's face would not change, the same set blank expression would greet them.

"I am fine."

"Good, good. Very good. Well, there's this to prepare and that to wash down and don't forget the beer we ordered which will arrive some time in the afternoon. You will need to put that in the cool store. You could perhaps ask the men to carry it up the stairs for you."

And the brush would be taken up, and the chopping knife, and Eva would set to work for another day. She was well looked after here, that was for sure.

She got her food too, you see. She could eat whatever she wanted. There were the bar *tapas* and there was bread, and some salads that didn't get used up; even, sometimes, a tortilla. She was allowed two short breaks to eat – "You must eat for the little one too!" – and to drink a cooling glass of water or a coffee. They also let her have a small room in their own apartment over the bar.

"You may sleep here," said the owners, "but in return we will expect you to clean the house for us – oh, and we would like you to do our washing and ironing. You needn't pay us any rent."

This was such an agreeable place to work, only a fool wouldn't see that. Living and eating for free, and a nice, bright modern bar to sweep and clean each day. There were no days off in the season, but Eva enjoyed the cleaning and the preparing – what else was life about? Through that long, boiling summer she scrubbed and polished the bar until it was spotless; you really could have eaten off the shining floors.

They paid her too; she got a wage on Sundays. They would not believe the amount she got, back in Mindanao – nearly two thousand pesetas a week. But the Philippines seemed a long way off now, a strange and different life. Eva hardly thought about it. Just a pity that her boy friend had gone away; she hadn't heard anything for a while now.

"I'll write," he had said. "I'll write you from the city. There are good jobs there – we could get a husband-and-wife position and live in. You'll see. Be patient, just wait."

So Eva waited, but it didn't seem that he could have found anything yet. Perhaps by the time the child was born he would have come for her.

The lump moved in her belly; a glimmer flashed in the brown-black eyes and Eva smiled. It was getting big, this creature; she could feel what must be a small foot arching out to the perameters of its dim, muffled world, dabbing at her stomach. Gently, she stroked the place where it had reminded her of itself.

"Limones! Madre Dios, mujer, necesitamos limones!"

The brown-black eyes dulled, the smile faded, the miniature foot retreated into its lair, and the patient, yellow-brown hand took up the chopping knife. Lemons for the customers' drinks we need.

Swop! Swop!

Tartly juicy thin yellow slices fell evenly, neatly, precisely beneath the steady steel blade. The tangy fluid spilled, and also the pips, to be wiped swiftly and efficiently away. Next the salad – put out the olives, spread the tuna. So it was, every hour of every day. It was safe this routine; she lived, she ate, she had a bed to sleep in, and she knew it well. She was indeed so very protected, so very fortunate. Tonight, she must get the ironing done. It was piling up in the close, shuttered apartment where she would sit for about an hour in the later evening. Occasionally she would watch the big colour television or a video, as the owners were either out somewhere else or chatting sociably with their regular customers in the bar. But the programmes did not interest her, and mostly she would sit quite still, silent, expressionless. She was not sad, and she was not happy. She was simply in her own space. So they sweated through the hot months, Eva and the bump. The little thing was restless, expanding, wanting more space than her short-hipped body could provide; and so it pushed uncomfortably outwards and she had to walk in this lumbering, paddle-footed fashion with the great swelling stuck on the front of her like a bad joke.

"My goodness, look at the size of you, girl!" Gonzalo, the new barman, would tease."We can put the customers' beer on that if we run out of tables!"

Eva would smile, faintly, her wide bland mouth lengthening just slightly. Her back ached more these days and she thought only of the overflowing laundry and ironing baskets in the apartment. The bar was extra busy these days: custom had grown. The Cafe-Bar Prima had won the Golden award for the best-kept, cleanest bar on the south Costa, and the one with the most varied menu, so they came from great distances to stand and drink in it, or to eat the Malaysian delicacies that Eva had learned from Bernard before he went away. On Sundays she never stopped, and as the heat shimmered over the white concrete roads and the bump moved irritably inside her sweating body, Eva would stand over the stove and feel her eyes, her legs, her arms so heavy, so very heavy, with the mass of her belly pressing downwards onto her swollen thighs.

But she was lucky. She had this place to live and plenty to eat – there was even some chicken left over this weekend, a real treat. Of course, there was always rice. And they were nice to her, the owners of the bar. They would praise her for those special efforts, the exotic food that drew the clients, and they would force her to stop working for ten minutes and eat her own meal.

"Have more bread, Eva. You're feeding for an army, by the looks of things. Here, this wants using up – it'll only go stale. You take it."

But Eva's dry mouth would clart up and she could think only of fruit, fresh, cooling, fleshy fruits, huge ripe water melons and oranges that dripped juice, grown under the reliable Andalusian climate, that she didn't have time to shop for here. On such days it would seem that the sun would always be liked this, poised right over their heads to shoot its vicious rays to sear the earth, blanch the grass and wither the trees. Red, perspiring tourists would come gasping into the bar for relative coolness, shade and an iced beer. Eva, she did not sit out in the sun, even in her break times. She would go up to the store-room, which was quiet, and sit near the cooling cabinets where the stocks were kept. This was much better. She did not care about the sun, about life outside; she cared only about getting through this scorching day and the next, and the one after that.

But at last the blessed, short autumn came. September, and storms; the bump, now more a collection of angles and shapes, twitched and kicked its small, strong limbs as Eva hunched herself away from the crash of thunder and the fierce jagged lightning in the night.

October, and the calm warm days with the fresher breeze blown in from the Atlantic and cooler nights. The bump was fully grown, straining the pink overall to button-bursting so that Eva had had to sew a placket into it and get some safety pins. And then, quite suddenly, it decided it wanted to be born.

Eva was in the kitchen at the time, slicing tomatoes. The steady hand clenched the knife more strongly, the calm sallow face creased a little and her breath shortened into a sharp, soft panting. Otherwise you would not have known anything was different. There was just time to get her to hospital as her waters broke. An hour later, and she had her baby. Labour was very restful. One lay down, opened the legs, and unruffled, without fuss, the brown eyes wide and fixed, Eva pushed and panted hard and the tiny girl, face like a beautiful Buddha, slid out. Then they were put together in a clean, white hospital bed. It was very serene and nice, being off her feet all this time.

"Well done!" cried the nurses, relieved at not having had to do anything. Such an easy native birth. "She's adorable, your little daughter! What are you going to call her?"

But Eva smiled, and wept briefly for both joy and sorrow and said nothing. The nurses shrugged and walked away.

Late that evening, Eva returned by taxi to the apartment with her bundle. It was very quiet. The baby took the breast, and they both slept. Next day, the announcement was made.

The Cafe-Bar Prima got a lot of glory from this event, and the owners said laughing that they would put a picture of the child next to the photograph of themselves receiving the Award of Gold in Madrid. Our talisman, they said, our lucky little one. Customers showered the mother with gifts. Like a pale madonna, Eva sat heavy-eyed and received them. She was very tired.

"Una tesora!" cried the visitors. "A treasure! Such wonderful eyes- and look at all that hair!"

The treasure wanted for nothing. Even the regular English customers, the ones who were still there after the tide of tourists had washed over the town and ebbed, brought things. It was most surprising. Eva felt strangely stunned.

* * *

Two days later, Eva's return to work was requested.

"But I am extremely tired," she said, in a rare vocal ex-

158

plosion. "I am not ready to work again."

"You must. We cannot afford to pay you and lose your services whilst we employ someone else."

The bar owners – they had only recently returned from a foreign holiday tour, you see, and were really quite weary themselves and thus could not possibly take on all of Eva's duties – remained adamant.

"A week." Eva stood in front of them, clutching the treasure, stocky in her flat, wide shoes, the deep eyes shining with a rare mettle. She could feel her breasts leaking again, and wanted to be alone. "I will return in a week."

At that moment the treasure opened its diminutive maw and let out the hideous, relentless screech of the new-born. It clawed desperately for the precious milk supply.

"Very well," said the owners, hastily. "But not later than next Monday morning. This will cost us a great deal of money, and we want you to realise that we are only doing this as a favour to you because you have been with us for some time."

So Eva had her rest. She was lucky to have such kind bosses, was she not? For many employers would simply have sacked her. They really were being very nice to her.

For a further six days, therefore, she lived alone in the apartment, feeding, washing and holding her daughter, occasionally taking a little walk outside in the mild late autumn air; and if the tears fell from time to time when she thought of the baby's father, well, she could expect to feel a bit blue so soon after the birth.

It was a strange time, this, but a good one. She got to know the exact length of every segment of each small finger, every little crease in the plump buttocks, the slightest noise and chunter the baby made. It was a hiatus of peace; there wasn't even any ironing to do, as the owners had been away a month and Eva had left everything in the place laundered before the birth. It was like a holiday, one could say, but then she remembered the holiday she had had in Seville with Bernard; a fortnight, when they'd first been together. The stupid tears came again, and Eva pushed them away with an angry hand. There was nothing to be sad about. She had her baby, a good place to live, and people had been so kind; so very, very kind. Many were not so fortunate.

Work came easily after that. The treasure lay in its coton-wheels in the corner of the bar, and Eva would slip discreetly out to feed at intervals, opening her overall and attaching the pink bud of a mouth firmly round an erect brown nipple. She would gaze at the suckling black head with silent pride. Deftly, the other nipple was offered, a nappy changed. The treasure went back to its pram-cot, Eva to her mop and dishcloth, and then the chopping and slicing. Really it was all very simple. The little thing was very content and would lie staring at the bright colours of the bar, the shiny bottles and the gaudy plastic vines, and make enchanting noises. One or other of the owners would often lift up the child and carry her round for the customers to see.

"Our bar baby," he would say, laughing, and the infant would burp cutely and obligingly over his shoulder and make them all laugh. Gay men are often very good in this way.

"Que guapatita!" they could cry again. "Que tesora!"

More drinks would be ordered to toast the new arrival's health and, merely as an incidental, the future success of the Cafe-Bar Prima.

Hands would reach out for a turn to hold the precious creature; more gifts arrived. The treasure was swamped with white and pink frilly dresses, matinee coats, bootees and intricately decorative shawls, all laced with pink ribbons. An English lady, a regular now, brought strange things – brilliant yellow dungarees and a vibrant red striped stretch suit; these Eva put carefully in a drawer. It was a tranquil time, and really the additional work was not so bad now that the weather was cool, and the bump was outside instead of in. One's body was one's own again, and one did not sway around in that wearying, waddling fashion. It was just this ridiculous habit she had of bursting into tears over nothing. Nobody could understand it, least of all Eva herself. But these little moments of crisis would soon pass, and they learned to ignore them.

"A nursing mother often gets a bit emotional," the man from the Guardia Civil said as he sipped his evening cognac. "My wife had six, and after every one my life was hell for nearly a year."

"I know what you mean." Another nodded, wisely. "My sister-in-law is giving my brother a real hard time just now – doesn't know what she wants from one moment to the next!"

"Women!" said the thinner of the bar owners. "First they want babies, then they seem to be miserable and moody once they get them. And really, kids are the easiest thing in the world. I mean – look at that."

The men craned their necks to peer at the cot-on-wheels, where the treasure – a rather bigger one by now – lay placidly kicking its legs and trying to grab its pink bootees. Smiles and sighs went round the bar. Eyes grew unashamedly moist.

"Los ninos – siempre son regalas de Dios!"

Further cognacs were poured on the strength of this sentiment, and the health of all these miraculous gifts from heaven was drunk with fervour.

One day, when the treasure was trying to sit up in her pram, the fatter of the two bar owners, who had grown very stout during this prosperous year, called Eva to him.

"I don't want you to waste time cleaning the men's toilets three or four times a day. I've noticed you spend a lot of time doing that."

"But... they get... soiled."

Eva was embarrassed. How to tell this gross creature that he, amongst others, spilled urine on the tiled floor whenever he used the lavatory? It was unhygienic, and it stank.

"Don't argue with me, girl. I'm the boss, and you do as I say."

"But the regulations – "

"And I tell you that twice a day is more than enough – morning and last thing. Is that clear? Now, go and get on with something else."

What had got into the girl? Normally she uttered hardly a word, getting on with her work silently and, it had to be admitted, efficiently. But since this baby business, well, she had begun to answer back at times. The heavy face trembled with annoyance. Women's moods!

The large, inflated body – bigger than Eva's bump at its full extent – heaved itself round the bar. Eva stood in the middle of the floor, mutely rebellious, the full lipped mouth clamped shut. The treasure began to yell, sensing something bad in the air. The fat one looked up sharply.

"Don't go to her now. She's getting older and she'll have to learn to wait for your attention."

He spread a fleshy arm across the bar counter, across the lift-up flap so that Eva could not get through. She stared at him. The treasure continued to howl. The fat bar owner stared back: the impasse seeming insurmountable. But then, by some miracle, the yelling abated.

"You see?" said the owner, triumphantly. "Just attention seeking. There's nothing wrong with her."

Without a word, Eva turned and continued her work behind the counter. Swop! Swop! Went the chopping knife with extra force, squirting lemon juice viciously across the board. Crunch! grunted the onions, oozing out their stinging spray. The treasure, subdued by some sixth sense, sucked the thumb of one hand and twisted the light cover in the small fingers of its other into a tight twist, and a heavy silence fell in the bar.

Later that week, and into the next, they had a rush of customers. There was a religious holiday, fiestas in the towns. Good-natured drunkenness was rife and the men's toilet was quickly awash with piss. Eva's scrupulous nature, her impeccable standards, could not stand the sight. For the third time that morning she took up her mop, the disinfectant and a bucket. All the food had been prepared, and there was a quantity of ice and lemons for the drinks.

"What are you doing, girl?"

A massy shadow blocked the doorway, blocking out the light from the bar. Eva looked at him sullenly.

"I am cleaning the toilet."

"But I told you not to. Once in the middle of the morning, once at night – it's sufficient. So long as it is clean at the busiest period and at the end of the day."

"Not when we are this busy. It is not enough. It is disgusting."

"Nonsense! That floor is perfectly clean. Look at it yourself."

"Because I have just done it. Before, it was covered with … well, you should smell what is in the bucket for yourself."

She thrust the muddy, reeking water towards him, and the large body edged away its bulk.

"Very well, very well. Just today, when we are so crowded. But if I catch you again wasting time on this, and getting yourself not fit to prepare food, look at your face all sweaty and your hands stinking of bleach, I will be very angry. Now wash, and get to the kitchen."

But the following day was the same. A lot of customers, and none of them seemed to be able to aim very well. Eva held herself back, bit her tongue, gritted her teeth, clenched her jaw. All morning she was aware of the seeping, unpleasant odour from the lavatory. You couldn't smell it in the bar, that was true, but in the kitchen it was quite apparent. The treasure was moody that day, bawling for feeds at times that were inconvenieint, failing to enchant as it usually did, though several maternal customers took it in their arms to try to still its fractiousness. The best at this was the quiet English lady who had given the loudly coloured and striped garments, and who took the little creature outside onto the patio and rocked it for long enough, out of sight and sound of the bustling, hectic hot air of the bar. This Englishwoman had no children of her own, it seemed; maybe the treasure sensed her deprivation, and clung to her and sobbed only quietly, snuffling its damp Buddha nose into her blouse in a sort of sympathy. For this, Eva was grateful.

At two o'clock, she could bear it no longer. She took up her bucket, rubber gloves and the disinfectant. Ten minutes later, and Eva's tidy, ordered soul was appeased, the toilets sparkling and sweetly smelling. She sat on her heels, looking at her work with quiet satisfaction.

And now, a swingeing blow caught her sideways across the head, sending her off balance so that she fell against the wooden partitition and bruised her forehead. A hard fist grasped her arm and yanked her to her feet.

"I thought I told you not to do that again?"

The wobbling face, darkling with anger, was so close to her that she could see the sweat running down the bulbous cheeks. Eva pulled herself away from him, backed into a narrow cubicle.

"Fat pig!" She hardly knew what she was saying, she did not remember that she was so lucky to be working here, that they had all been so nice to her, that she had plenty to eat and a good place to sleep. She forgot it all.

"You leave me alone, or I will tell the Police that you hit me. And you don't get me the proper employment papers. I will tell them about that too, and other things! You leave me alone."

The heavily flushed face pushed itself forward again to her own, the small eyes malicious behind the thick-lensed glasses.

"Oh you will, will you, stupid damn Filipina? Well you just look out for the safety of your beloved baby, that's all."

And he thrust his fist in front of her bunched in menace.

Eva sprang like a cat, her hands clawing at him, at anywhere she could reach, spitting like an animal and cursing him in her own language.

"You evil devil! You fat, evil hog!"

Easily, contemptuously, the bar owner fended her off, and with another glancing swipe at her pallid face, walked off to his station behind the bar.

"Get back to the kitchen," he said, hissing the words over his shoulder so that they could not be heard by the drinking throng. "And don't defy me again."

Eva stood where she was, fingering the red hand-mark on her already swelling cheek. Tears scalded down her face, and she cried silently, wretchedly, until sense returned and she cleared away the cleaning things. But she did not want to go back into the kitchen. Instead, she walked out to the patio, where the English lady still walked with the baby. Eva held out her arms for her treasure, her gift from God, and clutched the small being to her. The English lady took her arm, sat her down in a plastic patio chair, sat down opposite her, covered Eva's wrists with her own warm, fair hands. They said nothing. One could do nothing, that was the problem. Nothing at all.

* * *

Several weeks later, the English lady was in the bar again.

"Hola, Senora Patricia!" Gonzalo grinned in his customary, cheerful way. "We haven't seen you for a while."

"I've been in England."

"Ah! England. Was it nice?"

"So-so. It rained a lot."

"It always rains in England, they say."

"Well – not quite all the time. People exaggerate about England."

The English lady sipped her coffee. There was a silence she did not associate with the Cafe-Bar Prima.

"It's very quiet in here this evening," she said. "Where is everybody?"

Gonzalo pointed to a postcard, garishly coloured and depicting pyramids, with a camel posed carefully in the foreground.

"The owners are away again – They've gone on vacation to Egypt. It was very hard work over the summer, and they needed the break."

"Oh. I see. How – nice for them."

The English lady pushed her cup forward and Gonzalo refilled it, the saucer and the spoon making an empty clattering in the deserted bar. The kitchen door opened, and a pretty Spanish girl manoeuvred a large platter of salad round the counter. The English lady stared in surprise.

"Where is Eva? And the baby?"

Gonzalo shrugged.

"Oh, her boyfriend came one day. There was some trouble. The Police also came and the owners were accused of treating her badly and employing her illegally. But it was all settled."

The English lady pulled up a bar stool, noticed absently that it dragged several cigarette butts and matches with it, that the floor was obscured by a fine haze of dust.

"How do you mean? How was it settled?"

"Well, she'd been behaving strangely ever since the birth, you know. Temperamental, moody, having arguments with everyone – we just couldn't make her see sense. The Police dropped the charges in the end. After all, this bar has a first-class reputation. It has the Golden Award."

"But what did Eva do? I see you have a new girl."

"Oh Eva. She left. Her boy friend took her to the city."

"Has he got a job? A place for them?"

"Who knows? She didn't say much, just took her things one afternoon without warning and went. You want some tapas?"

"Please."

Gonzalo busied himself at the bar, and the English lady sipped her drink. Another silence hung in the air. Gonzalo felt it, and became uncomfortable. He leaned across the counter.

"It's not good you know, for someone to say so little as that one. She'd never talk with anyone. It's not normal. There was always something a bit odd about her.."

The English lady said nothing for a moment. Then,

"She must have been through a difficult time, though. Having the baby on her own and -"

Gonzalo beamed enthusiastically, his hands spread out towards this nice lady.

"That's exactly what we all said! The Police, even they agreed. Having the child in that way just unsettled her completely. In fact, we said we thought she'd gone a bit funny in the head." Meaningfully, he tapped his own forehead.

The English lady did not reply to this, but gazed at her distant, pale foreign image in the bar mirror. Gonzalo felt that more was called for.

"I mean, she always used to say how lucky she was to work here, how nice we all were. And she was, you know, very, very lucky. She used to say it herself. Only God nows how it might have been otherwise." Gonzalo pursed his lips, whistled softly, and with a serious expression rubbed hard at a streak of grease on the senora's table.

The English lady said nothing, but drained her coffee and excused herself. She wanted an early night, she said. Nor did she finish her tapas; it did not taste fresh, and had congealed on the dish.

After she had gone, in the quiet emptiness of the bar, Gonzalo polished the counter again, and the coffee machine, and the glasses, he cleaned them extra shiny with a white starched tea towel so that they glinted and flashed under the glare of the lights. Meanwhile he hummed to himself, and whistled again, as there was no-one to talk to. Marianna had gone home, as there was no need for her to stay; custom had fallen off lately. It would pick up again in the season.

"Yes," he said to nobody but the radio, gibbering endlessly in the background. "It was definitely the baby that unsettled her."

168

THE WANDISH PARTY

Mrs. Sehr Mayan studied the notice carefully. Read it three, four times, just to be sure. The printing was by hand, in Amira's careless capitals, and you couldn't always tell what her announcements said, but the heading was plain in enough in this instance, its lettering tall and bold against the white, like winter trees in England.

"Come to a Wandish Party! August 5th, 6.30 pm, Amira's house. All welcome." And then it instructed, in slightly smaller letters, "Sign below."

Mrs. Sehr sighed. It was very puzzling. She could not ask the others, however; that would be to display the most terrible and possibly ludicrous ignorance. Nor could she ask Amira herself; that could be interpreted as offensive.

In this small, remote settlement in the desert, where the new white concrete had sprung up and formed low, square houses and the greenery was forced into growth through miles of hose pipes and the tireless efforts of round the clock gardeners, such matters had to be handled with the greatest delicacy. There was so little to occupy the mind and the energy here and people, inevitably, talked. About anything of the least remark; about anyone. Mrs. Sehr did not want to be talked about. Obviously therefore, she must find out for herself just what a Wandish Party was, or might be. If one should do anything special; how much one should dress up – for one always did put on something nice for even a modest social occasion in someone's house, there being little else – other than the wonderful and eagerly anticipated Eid celebrations – to mark the calendar month by month throughout one warm, slow sleepy year after another.

They had been here twelve of these dozing years, the Mayans, and had therefore seen the influx of more workers in the plants that financed the town: the Asians, families from the various countries dotted across the Arab strip of the southern edge of the northern hemisphere, some from the Far East, or Eastern Africa, and a few pale, pinkish westerners who made uneasy friendships, stayed more briefly, and mostly left. Mrs. Sehr and her husband were set to remain; India, not far away, was yet very far away, and less and less did she miss the place.

But there was work to do; she must get on with her job and not stand staring at the notice board. Anwar would know; Anwar knew most things. This Mrs. Sehr had accepted on the day of their marriage thirty years ago when they saw each other for the first time in the Delhi suburb of her parents' home.

"A Wandish Party," Anwar would say authoritatively – Anwar with his high, balding head that had been so even on the youthful photo he had sent his arranged bride, that had shone out somewhat less aggressively at the wedding itself, but which had progressed gently into virtual hairlessness ever since, "yes, such a party is a commonly held event. It is..."

Comforted in the certainty of acquiring knowledge, Mrs. Sehr returned to the pile of patient files on her desk. It was, as always, a busy day, half of the township seeming to want to see a doctor at that particular hour, and the telephone constantly ringing with what appeared to be the other half too sick to get to the clinic. A typical day, in fact.

"It is the pollution from the plant," Nurse Tadqees would state, wisely, and heads would nod. "It makes us all ill."

Mrs Sehr would look at the shining dark eyes of the children as they vigorously ran about in the sun, the smooth, plump faces of the mothers, the strong, tall figures of the fathers in their white robes or salwar khameez and doubted this, but she would incline her head with the rest; one did not want to be out of step.

In just this way, one did not want to be wrong-footed at the Wandish Party; oh dear, thought Mrs. Sehr, there I go worrying about it again. Firmly, she pushed the problem onto the image of her husband; at thirty-two when they married, he had already been extremely knowledgeable, well read and refined, and now, when she herself was more than that and he well ahead of her, he could be expected to take charge of this dilemma. Still, it was baffling.

Likewise, others of the staff with whom Amira worked pondered the concept in nonplussed silence.

One or two attempted an obscure reference to the wording of the notice, casually bringing it into conversation as if they were familiar with it, and at the same time trying to elicit from someone else what it was all about. Rahima, young and still a junior nurse, had grown up in distant, chilly England. Her dress, on occasions, was not appropriate. She had predilection for skirts with rather long splits at the back, and her sweaters could be a little tight. It was hoped fervently by everyone that her engagement to a young doctor would calm her down, though he did not seem to be insisting, as surely he should, that she put on the scarf to cover her abundant, raffish hair, which continued to cascade flamboyantly down her back when it fell out of the clips and swept patients' notes onto the floor.

"Perhaps it is to do with wizards and conjurors," suggested Rahima, one hoped facetiously, and rather spilling the beans as to the fact that she didn't understand the notice either and didn't care who knew it. "Maybe we should all go in fancy dress. Maybe there will be tricks and magic."

Her colleagues looked at her sideways, and sideways they glanced at each other. She had that strange sense of humour peculiar to the cold group of islands in which she had – unfortunately, they often thought – been raised. God speed the wedding, children, and all such civilising influences.

However, Rahima could, they had to admit, just as easily have been right as wrong. Other ideas sprouted like vegetables in spring.

"Perhaps it is something political?"

"Or maybe something to do with the faith, that we women should be aware of?"

"No, I don't think that can be the case. After all, there are Christians on the staff too. Also Hindus and even a Sikh."

All the ladies sighed in unison. Though they welcomed the newcomers from different parts of the globe, that was one of the problems of living in this tiny – what did they call it? Microcosm? – with so many nationalities, religious practices (confusingly, the Christians seemed to have several), languages, expectations and customs, all clumped together like a badly gathered bunch of flowers and grasped in the fists of the companies who ran the industries. Forced, like flowers, to survive together in the same water, as it were, whether Muslim, like Amira, Hindu, like Mrs. Mahendran and her family, Coptic Christian as some of the Egyptians were, or Catholics from the Far East or Kerala... Could any water, however pure, nourish and satisfy them all?

Well, it had to; or rather, they had to take the best out of it. The women got together, of course, unable by custom or rules to go where the men could, to swim publicly with their own children, to visit the western style hotels at the beach, to ride a bicycle or enjoy mixed company other than close family; and so, bound by common constraints and the necessity of communicating in a tongue which was at best a second if not a third language for them all, they entertained each other. Carpets were rolled up, chairs pushed to the wall, head coverings, veils and dupattas abandoned and the dancing would start, each woman delighting in another's beauty and skill, as the hips twisted, the bosoms shook and the music urged them on. Such were their usual social gatherings.

But – a *Wandish* party?

The menfolk were consulted.

"What do you think, Anwar?" said Mrs. Sehr, having relayed the notice.

Frowning, her husband pushed his spectacles onto that beaming crown, rattled his newspaper briskly. She had caught him on the hop. His well-stocked mind searched the many slots into which he had poked chips of information, over the years, much as a computer whizzes through its data: history, art, science, literature, technology, world events and, of course, religion.

"Yes," he said, feeling his wife's steady trusting eyes upon him. "Mm, I think I know this word. Let me see."

With an outward appearance of assurance and an inner sense of desperation, Anwar pulled out the slips of knowledge he had on religious faiths – principally Islam, of course.

"So?" said Mrs. Sehr gently, with the understanding of more than a quarter of a century of living with this man; it was better not to push.

She remembered the weeks of trembling fear before her marriage, the unpropitious photograph which showed not only a lack of hair but a prominent forehead, somewhat bulging eyes and what looked horribly like a sneer to the mouth. In fact, the man in the flesh was considerably better, which proved to Mrs. Sehr that the pundits were wrong: the camera could, and often does, indeed lie. The marriage had gone well, or at least tolerably so, with only the little ups and downs that are universal to the married state. He was a quiet man, serene in nature, and kind. If he had one fault, it was this only: pride. She knew better than to put the merest pinprick in her husband's good opinion of his intellect, his self-worth.

So –

"So?" – quietly, like the merest outgoing of a breath, like the settling of a feather.

"It must be something to do with the run-up to Ramadan," said Anwar, having scanned his entire and prolific vocabulary in vain; the word simply did not exist, in English, Arabic, Hindi, Urdu or anything else so far as he could tell. "At least, that is my opinion," he added. "Probably," he further offered, being a man bound if not to tell the absolute truth on all occasions, at least to temper a lie.

"Ah. That would make sense." His wife's forty-three-year-old face, mildly scarred by the smallpox she had unhappily contracted three months before the wedding, relaxed. "Amira is having a party to celebrate the coming of the Holy Month, before we all start the fasting. I see."

The question only remained: what to do, what to take for the hostess? Not a gift until the Eid-Al-Fitr, surely? Mrs. Sehr and her conscience-stricken husband dwelt long on this point, before reaching their decision.

* * *

In Devi's house things were rather different. They had lived in America, and the effect on Devi, thought her husband, had been less than desirable. Bold-eyed, she looked men in the face and liked to talk on equal terms, as did those brash brassy females in Detroit. Oh, she dressed modestly enough, with the traditional long saris and salwars of conservative India, and even covered the upper part of her arms, the delights of her smooth, silky skinned shoulders quite properly only visible, let alone touchable, to him. But it was her attitude that didn't fit. She might as well have dyed her hair bright blonde and smoked cigarettes, she was so forward, so – *self confident*. It made him cringe and he noticed with chagrin that their daughter was heading the same way; at eight years old she could put out her tongue with the best of them and speak to him in a way that made him want to slap her.

Now this business of the Wandish party was the topic of the household; as if he hadn't plenty to think about, with the annual shut-down of the plant imminent and a batch of new workers to accommodate for its reactivation. Why couldn't these women just get on with their own affairs, gossiping and tripping over to each other's houses and doing whatever they did there? He didn't mind the expenditure on a new dress, a hairdo, the usual expenses of entertaining, but just leave him out of anything to do with it, please, so that he could go down to the men's club and get on with the important matters in life.

"Look, I don't care what kind of party it is," he said in exasperation. "Just don't go mentioning it again. I am sick of the thing."

Not for the first time, he thought with longing of Mumbai, where was his family: mother, father, aunts, uncles, cousins, nephews, nieces and even an ancient grandparent, and where all was familiar and unproblematic. Here, Devi all too often led him a dance, not being under the surveillance of their respective elders.

"Let us drop the subject," he said again, and put on his sandals to go out into the cooler, sweet desert evening air.

His wife arched her eyebrows at his back and in retaliation rang her sister in America to talk it over on the landline phone, instead of their usual Facebook contact, and stayed on the line for well over two hours. The bill, when it came in later, gave Dipesh a terrible attack of indigestion and he maintained thereafter that it was the start of a lifelong problem with ulcers. But Devi had her answer, winging through the curves of space with those strange breathy pauses you get on satellite calls, and it was with a secretive, complacent smile that she went to work at the Clinic the next day.

Though nothing was said, by now it was apparent that there was confusion and doubt about the nature of this party; nobody would admit it, but they were all, in their own ways, quizzing one another. Devi's self-satisfied smirk did not go unnoticed, but she would not be drawn.

"Don't ask me, please," she would say. "I don't know any more than you do."

If others didn't have sisters in America, that was their problem.

* * *

There were now eighteen names on the list. Two days to go, and most were still in a state of panic. It was crucial that they got it right. Social slips in so limited a place could glare like a lighthouse beam, shining on the perpetrator of the offence and making her, or him, the object of much comment and unfavourable judgement. At least, until the next faux pas.

"I don't believe this," moaned Amel, fingering the cross on the gold chain that she wore as a sign of her creed and in memory of her mother. "A party, in the house of one of my senior colleagues, and I don't know how to honour it.

176

What should I do?"

It happened that the mother-in-law was in the house, visiting from Alexandria, a stout woman who did not let a day pass without bewailing the family's fate that her eldest son should have married for love, and for love of this dumb creature who was not even Coptic, but something call *Anglican*. And now the stupid girl was bothering her with questions about something called a Wandish Party. Mrs. Aftab's English was not extensive, and she thought Amel's questions idiotic, even when put into Arabic, but she did not wish to offend her son, so kept most of her thoughts to herself.

Aloud, she said, "There is an answer to this. It is just a matter of thinking until we get to it."

"But where to start?" frowned Amel, justifiably perplexed.

"Oh, girl!"

Mrs. Aftab hawked in irritation. Really, Amel was undeniably extremely pretty, and just at this time heavily pregnant with the first grandchild, most likely a boy, as Mrs. Aftab's expert eye assessed the low-slung bump, but totally lacking in wits. However, as her son was not blessed in the looks department, though of high intelligence, she was not displeased to have an injection of beauty into the family line. She looked forward to a child who inherited his mother's splendid, regular features and fine eyes, and his father's brains. This silly young woman couldn't think what to do for a party, just because it had been given a fancy title; undoubtedly the pregnancy had made her even more bird-witted than usual.

"Here's what you should do." She leaned towards her daughter-in-law in that female conspiracy so bewildering to their men, and whispered.

"Are you sure?" Amel widened the fawn-eyes further,

177

and her mother-in-law stared into their brilliant but empty depths with impatience.

"Of course. Come on, girl. We must go to the supermarket."

* * *

In fact, the Novela market did very well that week. It saw brisk trading, which puzzled the manager, as Ramadan was still ten days away, and generally the rush did not start till a couple of days before, when he would keep open the store until midnight or later, and people would pile high their trolleys with every known item of food, every delicacy in stock, so that the place would assume the jollity of a gala: nobody wanted to be caught short in providing for the *Iftar* at the end of a long day's fasting, or for the last meal, just before sunrise.

But now? Was there something he had not been told about? What was going on?

The ladies remained distant, discreet, those behind their veils more impenetrable than ever, those with faces uncovered checking through the tills with unaccustomed speed. Nabil was affronted; as a rule, he was among the first to know what was going on in the town, in the swim of things as it were. However, he shrugged. Life here was too easy-going and the climate impossible in these summer months, much too hot to stay on high dudgeon about anything, and besides, it looked like mere women's stuff. Not of great interest, therefore, to a man of his status in the community.

All the same.

"That's a lot of booty you've got there," he said, and, "My, my, I'll have to phone the warehouse again," or, "Are you starting up in competition at your house? You'll soon have more of my supermarket there than I have."

But the ladies of the Clinic merely smiled like the Cheshire Cat Nabil remembered reading about somewhere as a child, and he got no further.

"What are those women up to this week?" he said at the men's club, as his friends treated him to another Turkish coffee and they smoked together.

"I've no idea," said Wafiq off-handedly. "But if it keeps them happy and out of our hair, why should we worry?"

This was true, and since Novela's cash registers were pinging merrily in their computerised way, why indeed should Nabil lose any sleep over it?

* * *

The day came. It was, as always, a fine day, with the relative freshness of the desert morning giving way to a warm mid-day and a long, sultry afternoon in which the town had its siesta and the streets were quiet and still, even the blue-garbed gardeners sleeping under the shade of the endlessly watered shrubs and trees. Children, hushed into drowsiness, rested to save their energies for the burst of evening activity which would take them up to their late bedtime, and the mosques were silent, as if holding their breath for the late afternoon call to prayer.

The Clinic closed its doors at lunch time; no evening session today, a Thursday. The Ladies scurried home, also to rest and then to prepare. In the silent time of the heat's crescendo, all that could be heard in the deserted streets was the thrumming of the air conditioning units as they tirelessly pumped refrigerated air into the quiet bedrooms, even the birds stilled and mute in the stifling haze. The sun swelled, as if gorging itself on the clearer air that floated in from the turquoise sea, sometimes curdling with the heat rising from the land to produce humidity so thick you could have sliced it up and served it on a plate; and it was not until gone seven that its flattened orb slipped with that ever-startling abruptness towards the wide, blank desert horizon behind the town. The white houses, the sandy tracks, the tarmac roads all seemed to melt into rose-gold; the waves sighed in level, tranquil rushes onto the beach, reclaiming the scattering of debris with the evening tide, and the muezzins roused the heavens with their husky call. The mosquitoes stirred and busied themselves for their nightly feasting and the crickets rubbed rowdily in the thick bladed grass. At eight o'clock, the guests wove their way from their various houses, a sluggish collection of rivulets which merged into a solid stream towards Amira's home. Each bearing something, each anxious, each hiding this from themselves and the others with their bright party smiles.

"Welcome!" Amira opened her door to the eighteen of them, and clapped her hands at the sight of one offering after another.

"Oh, Mrs. Sehr! How beautiful!"

"Amel, that is fantastic!"

"Devi, Rahima, Bushra... What a time we are going to have tonight!"

The eighteen offerings – and more, for some had brought two or three – were eagerly seized; the eighteen bearers, empty-handed and suddenly bereft of the slight security of clutching their gifts, looked at Amira. It seemed that they had done the right thing, at any rate; but was there anything else? Amira looked much as usual – slightly flushed, a bit of lipstick and yes, her best gold; the house clean and orderly and attractive as the Filipina maid always made it, but – they peered surreptitiously – no overt signs to indicate that the party represented anything exceptional, either socially or religiously.

180

Anxiously, the eighteen shuffled forward into the dining room. Sniffed. Stood uncertainly in the silence.

"Whatever is the matter?" cried Amira, clapping her hands once more. "You all look so miserable. This is a party. Come on!"

At last, hugely pregnant Amel, free of the deadening clutches of her husband's mother, spoke out for the reticent seventeen. Maybe it was the imminence of the birth – she went into labour fifteen hours later and had a girl who was neither particularly beautiful nor intelligent, thus confirming Mrs. Aftab's deepest prejudices against mixed marriages – maybe it was this that gave her a sort of dumb courage. Anyway,

"But Amira," she said, putting her hands solidly on the bump, "that's the point. I didn't know what kind of party it was to be, so I didn't know what I should do. Or what gift to bring."

A murmur went from the women to the left of her, to her neighbour, and to the women on her right. Like a contagion, the shaming confession spread.

"Nor I," muttered Devi. "Until I spoke to my sister," she added, as she liked to stress this point. "She is in America, you know."

"Even my husband was not really sure, now I come to think of it. And he has two degrees from the best universities." Mrs. Sehr recalled Anwar's slightly hesitant proclamations, and a little of the twenty-five-year-old deference crumbled; only a hairline crack, but it was a start.

One by one they fell, like bottles off a wall, in the unfortunate admission of Not Knowing.

"You did not realise?" Amira laughed, astonished. "You really did not know what a Wandish party is?"

"No."

"Oh my goodness. Where have you lived? It is something my English friend Patricia told me about – she was here last year, if you remember? In any case, it is exactly as you have all done – so how can you tell me you didn't understand about it?"

This was too much. Mrs. Sehr, taking control, seized Amira firmly by the shoulders.

"Tell us, because we did not know, and because we didn't, we have all, as you see, brought you something to eat. We have all cooked. One dish each or sometimes two."

"Pre-*cisely*."

The eighteen looked carefully at each other; at the extended table, where a collection of the most aromatic, steaming containers sat, each exuding its own unique and appetising smell from under the loosened foil covers. They looked at Amira, with her wide smile.

"One dish," she murmured. "Each person brings *one dish*."

Oh.

Oh, *oh*.

Rahima was the first to shriek, tossing back the long untidy swathes of hair.

"Aey-eee! Aaaah-eee!"

Amel swore that it was that, the sudden sharp screech without warning, that woke the foetus and started the early contractions, leading to the breaking of the waters in the night. The hullabaloo went round the nineteen of them – Amira as well – and back, and round again. Weeping followed, laughter hysterical and relieved, and they clung to each other. The great secret was out, the mystery was no more. Husbands were perceived to be not so great after all when it came down to it, themselves rather clever.

"A Wan-dish party, yes," breathed Mrs. Sehr, licking her fingers clean of Mrs. Raafat's excellent *koshiri*. "We must have one every year."

WE LIKE BEING MARRIED

JUSTINE WAS QUITE A bit older than her husband; eight years, to be exact, and that is a lot when it is that way round.

At forty, Wasim Hassan considered himself a desirable man, in the way that men are wont to do. As indeed he was. Tall, athletic, with his keen, bright, dark eyes and light olive complexion, not to mention his very good teeth which thanks to the French dentist in Casablanca were his own, he could have passed for thirty-two, and not a day over.

When he met Justine he was already divorced; in modern Casablanca, this was not unusual. The two children of this marriage he saw but irregularly. His Moroccan wife, still young, had moved away; he no longer saw her, no longer cared. Thus Wassim, affluent in his branch of the family business, elegant, well shod and generally successful, was free to roam as he pleased.

"I'm thinking of going to Spain for the holiday," he said to a friend. "It's the Spanish New Year. How about coming along?"

So the two of them went to Malaga, vibrant, shabby old city alive with popping children and fireworks, the Paseo Maritimo bulging with people and fiesta market stalls. Wasim and his friend – who was swarthy, smallish and plump and therefore no competition, and who in consequence furnished Wasim with the most comfortable of friendships, being totally uncritical of him – these two, they ate outside one of the street restaurants in the cool dry winter evening. It was here that he met Justine, a pretty, vivacious American. He did not think her forty-eight; perhaps forty, certainly not more.

Justine was very chic in a way that intrigued Wasim. Her shining dark red hair swung in a sharp bob round her well-boned face; her black skirt, just above the knee, clung softly to her long, slender legs in their fine silky black hose and her simple well-shaped large silver jewellery impressed itself upon the eye as a refreshing alternative to the ornate, overworked brassy gold favoured by the women of his own culture. Justine also had clear, pale skin and wonderful wide green eyes; a touch of subtle lipstick added the final shade to her palette. Her whole style was effortlessly effective. Wasim was enchanted.

She was a writer, she said, staying with friends in Spain and working on a collection of stories. In soft, sensual French, Wasim conversed with and wooed Justine; in broken, inexact French she charmed him.

"Come with me to Morocco," he urged her on their third night together. He ran his hand down her still-slim, still-vigorous fair body with its high breasts and long waist and hips. "Come and spend some time with me in my home. You will love it."

"Oh yes," said Justine, her green eyes closing together and her legs wound tightly round him in the ecstasy of it all.

After a few more days they went to Wasim's French-style apartment in Casablanca. The city was wonderful, the apartment perfect, Wasim's smart town friends were taken with her. Everything was just as it should be. The "some time" turned into a longer time, and there was no sign that either wanted to end it. Wasim, for his part, was pleased with his acquisition; a beautiful, intelligent American woman. Besides, she was unexpectedly easy to please. She needed little, she said – only a room with an inspiring view, lots of paper and an old fashioned electric typewriter. This was how she preferred to work. "Really writing," as she called it. Moreover, Justine could give her opinion on a number of things, but always with amiability, a gentle grace, so that Wasim never felt threatened as he had by so many women lately. Even his own sisters were beginning to contradict him, and as for his wife, she had taken umbrage and jibbed at a great many things he did and said, things that every man has a right to do or say.

Justine did none of these things, only smiled at him more and made love to him more ardently, lovingly and frequently. Wasim began to think that a lot of nonsense was talked about American women; those in his own country, these days, were far more aggressive and demanding.

"Marry me," he said on day over breakfast. Not expecting to be refused.

Justine had no intention of refusing. She had worked hard for this moment. How else could she, a woman alone, live as a writer in such a country as Morocco? If Wasim, and marriage to Wasim, was part of the bargain, she reflected, really it was a most acceptable one; she could get to the heart of things simply by being at his side. Justine knew that he had relatives in the more traditional area inland, which he liked to visit; Wasim was more Moroccan than he cared to think.

And besides, he was also beautiful. He was mostly good-natured (especially when free to do as he wished) and Justine did nothing to shake that equilibrium. In consequence, he was indulgent with her, genuinely affectionate. Perhaps she was just the smallest bit in love with him as well, which was no bad thing. Most of Justine was not in love with Wasim, and had never been in love with anyone in her life; in lust, yes, of course, but there was a still, cold centre to her – though it was not her heart. That beat warmly enough; Justine was no

Snow Queen. No, it was more a sort of watching eye which few suspected, hardly anyone saw. But it can be nice for a part of you to be in love, just so long as it is firmly disciplined and kept under surveillance by the rest; and it can even be useful.

In this way, Justine's in-love part was allowed to play, and the watchful eye allowed the marriage to take place.

"What are you writing, my dearest?" enquired her husband one day, some months after the wedding. Life had settled to a most satisfactory pattern.

"I'm working on some stories about Spain," returned Justine, placidly.

Wasim peered at the typed sheets. They were in English, naturally, in which he was not in the least proficient. He shrugged and smiled, trailed a finger down to Justine's well-formed behind and pressed it in the crease between her taut buttocks. He felt the pelvic bone tighten as she arched against him, and recalled the night before.

Later, he said, "Is there anything you want from the city? I am going to do some shopping this afternoon."

"No, my love," said Justine, smoothing the dusky stockings over those long legs. "But don't forget – we are dining with Laila and Louis Rafiq tonight."

The Rafiqs were a French-Moroccan couple, and Wasim liked to mix with them.

"Wear something elegant then, my darling," he said, "but also sexy."

Justine obeyed him to the letter. Her reddish hair, highlighted now with henna and fine gold strands, shone and swayed. Her lightly tanned honey skin glowed, and she took extra care with the make-up. The dress she chose was off-the-shoulder black, for this was Justine's best, better than all the rainbow for her green and white and red-gold colouring, and it silhouetted her tallish, American figure

186

to great advantage. The brocade heeled pumps and real, oyster pears (Wasim's birthday gift) completed what Justine had just written into one of her stories.

"*Sabina was dressed in that indefinable, expensively-kept-woman way,*" announced the sheet of paper in her typewriter.

"Hm," said Justine, musing at her reflection in the mirror. The green eyes there met the real with a certain glint. She blew her mirror image a little kiss.

"All part of the bargain," she said to it, "so you can just shut up."

And she took the powder brush and dusted on another translucent layer, just to be absolutely sure. *Fireproof,* she said to herself, and stored the word.

Wasim, of course, approved and they left the house in their usual accord. In the street outside the beggars lay like bundles of rags, wearied by what they were and what they would always be. Limbless, in some cases sightless, and inevitably hopeless, they observed dumbly as the tall, handsome, rich Arab and his slender, creamy-gold American wife, with her lovely, gently humorous face left the select apartment block, watched without expectancy as Wasim hurried Justine past their outstretched hands to the white Mercedes. It was beginning to be winter again, and the Atlantic sent in a cold mist that made the bones ache; inland, in the mountains, they said, there was frost. Wasim wrapped the short fur jacket more tightly round his wife.

"I hope the Rafiqs have their heating on," he said. "It's a pig of a night."

Justine was the hit of the evening. Many friends who had not previously met Wasim's new wife came up to congratulate him.

"You are a lucky dog," they hissed in his ear.

"What a prize! She is beautiful. Those legs!"

"And so charming. Such wit!"

Wasim inclined his head to receive these compliments, much as one being told he has the best camel in town.

"She is, you understand, somewhat older than I," he said, confidentially, to two of his closest friends.

"One would never suppose it. You both look eternally young. Long may it continue, by the will of Allah!"

* * *

And it seemed that it did please Allah that such a state of affairs should continue.

"Do you like being married to your old Moroccan, then?" Wasim would ask playfully, and she would give the expected reply.

"I love being married to you."

It was true; the arrangement suited Justine perfectly, and it was obviously true that it suited Wasim just as well.

He would go off to his business in the morning, lunch with friends, and return around seven in the evening, five or sometimes six days a week. This left Justine delightfully free to write, to read, to swim, to think and generally live in the way she had dreamed about for nearly twenty years. Wasim and his relations gave her the life of Morocco, and otherwise she lived her own. The freedom to be a writer was hers; and she was, at last, beginning to be successful.

This was just as well, for Wasim, a rich man, was careful with her money and gave her nothing. He kept her in supreme comfort, and she asked for little. Now and then he would take her on his arm and stroll round the more fashionable quarter of Casablanca; or perhaps, at her insistence, they would visit the Medinas in the older cities, to which he reacted with the distaste of a foreign tourist, the sort that suspects dysentery on every orange

188

and disease in the very particles of the air. On such occasions Wasim would press a handkerchief to his prominent nose, standing well back from whatever souq stall Justine had plunged into, refusing all offers to "Sit down, sir, my friend, come drink mint tea with me", until his wife would laugh at him, buy a pair of leather slippers or a rug for the sake of it, and then give in to his desire to rejoin the civilised world. Sometimes he would even take her across that narrow stretch of water, the chasm between two worlds, and they would go to Madrid, where it pleased Wasim to deck out his wife in the latest fashions. Twice, even, they got as far as Paris, but Wasim shivered in the light autumn rain and declared it a place without heart. English-speaking countries they never visited; for some reason, Wasim abhorred the language – "flat, no music in it" – and what he contemptuously called the cold pale English type, and so he mastered not a word of her mother tongue. This also suited Justine very well.

In the meantime, publishers' cheques were piling up in the bank account in Gibraltar of which Wasim had not the faintest knowledge and to which he had no access.

Occasionally Justine would make a trip across the Straits by herself; to visit friends, she said, and Wasim did not demur. She did and was all he wanted; left him to live his own life when he wished, did not enquire into his afternoons, those long, warm hours when even in January the sun was capable of a sudden, blowsy burst of sultry heat; and she pleased him when he wished to be pleased, their bed (and other locations) a realm of transport and mellow rapture. She should thus have a little freedom, yes; after all, he was a modern man and went to night clubs, he lived in Casablanca, not ancient Fes or out in the sticks at Oud Zem.

In this way, two years and more passed, and still neither Wasim nor Justine showed any signs of ageing. They would be sociable in the evenings, and on Fridays would go to the beach or into the country.

"Your wife is very lovely," his uncle Morad murmured on one such occasion. "She has such wonderful skin – and that hair! I cannot believe that she is more than fifty."

"Nor I," admitted Wasim, and went to put an arm, possessive and protective, around the smooth, slightly sun blessed ivory shoulders of his wife. At once the young man who had been telling her with fervour how utterly wonderful she was and that he was mad for her melted away like morning moisture on the desert cactus.

"Ha!" said Wasim. "I see I shall have to look out for rivals."

"You have none, and well you know it," said Justine frankly. Really, it was impossible not to love him with just that small, capricious, free-running part of her. She did, very much, appreciate being married to him.

So, then, Justine clattered through her days on the old, friendly typewriter on which she still preferred to tap out her scripts. She liked the sound, she said, and she would not, she affirmed, want to gaze at a lighted screen all day, refusing with graceful determination her husband's offer to buy her a computer, a state of the art laptop.

"Here I can sit on my balcony," she declared, "and type away, and still look at this wonderful view" – and she waved her arm to demonstrate her point – "and the sun will not melt my ancient machine nor obscure my reading of what I have done."

Wasim followed her gaze, over the white roofs of Casablanca to the calm sea, crested lightly with Atlantic surf, glanced up into the pale blue sky of a North African winter and heard the chattering rhythms of the street below. In that moment he saw and listened to his city through the eyes of his wife, realised the bird's-eye-view that Justine had from her nest high up on the apartment block, saw what he had forgotten, or, perhaps, immersed in it from childhood, had never seen.

"Very well, my darling," he said, and the matter was closed.

In the afternoon, while Wasim pursued his interests in the city – Justine suspected a little gambling, a little smoking of hashish, possibly a visit to a belly dancing venue, but wisely chose to ignore the hours from two till seven – then Justine would rest so that she could be fresh for his homecoming, so that there would be that sparkle for him in her green eyes. That much vanity had Justine, that much pride; and that much hard, self-preserving common sense.

For eight years is rather a lot, especially when one is sailing the wrong way from fifty, having docked at the port of middle age and begun, be it ever so gently, to head off towards another shore. Justine rested on the wind, tacked in her sails; her existence, here in this haven, after all depended on her looks, her continuing charm. She held herself, her muscles, tauter; ate sparingly, exercised; dressed cleverly, relaxed frequently and made sure the lights were low and diffused for love-making.

At last, as two or three more years span out their enchanted threads, at last she began to age. Just a little, at fifty-three and four; slightly faster at fifty-five, and then, at fifty-six, with a startling, accelerating suddenness that plummeted her into the heavy, cold waters of approaching old age. She was still remarkably attractive, of course; that sort of bone structure never alters, and she did not put on weight.

But –

"Isn't she wonderfully lovely – for her age," they said

now, and "she must have been really beautiful when she was young."

Wasim, not unaware of these remarks, began to come home later. Sometimes, even, he did not appear on days off. He was just as kind, affectionate and generally agreeable with her, but Justine knew that she had lost some part of him.

She had enough money of her own by now and an established reputation, so that she could go and live independently if she wished; her publishers and her agent had done her proud. But really, thought Justine, with a lowness of spirit, how could she bear to leave Morocco, and how and where could she live alone? Besides, she did still, very much, like being married to Wasim.

And still did he escort her on some evenings for their social engagements, but he did not rush to her side with that once-possessive arm. There was no need. Justine found herself talking to the older wives, or to their gallant but decrepit husbands. The dark, neat head of her own youthful husband she could just see across the room, but it did not turn her way. There was no need.

"Wasim," she said one night as they drove home. They had been married seven years. "Have you got another woman?"

The vehicle jerked, bucked and shuddered under Wasim's shocked hands as he stabbed at the brake pedal.

"Justine! How can you ask such a thing?"

"Because I want to know," she said sadly, in such a simple way that it brought the truth out into the open where neither of them could avoid it. There was a silence, broken only by the quiet spitting of light winter rain on the windscreen. Justine knew that it was up to her to prevent herself from falling into the abyss. She recalled the beggars at the foot of their apartment building, their pleading hands, the empty eyes. Am I like them? she thought. She must be very careful, very wise.

"Wasim, listen. I understand. I am not condemning you. I was aware that one day this would happen – how could I think otherwise? You are much younger than I, and still most desirable. How could you continued to be satisfied with so much older a wife? If you have a mistress, I shall not utter one word of complaint. Only I would prefer to know."

"Very well." Wasim was cold, embarrassed and somehow emasculated by this speech, by her generosity, her frank graciousness. "I have met another woman – a French woman, as it happens. She is thirty-two and yes, she is very pretty."

"What does she look like?"

"You really want to know?"

Wasim looked curiously at his wife. He found her attitude puzzling. Now his first wife, all fire and rage, would have flown at him like a maddened animal, clawed him to shreds and cursed him with every known epithet. He was unwilling to answer, and did not know what to say, how to handle this uncharted territory.

"I must know. Go on."

"As you wish." Wasim turned his head, stared out of the window at the dull night. He did not want to look at Justine while he said this. "Antoinette is blonde, not as tall as you, but with a good figure. She has large brown eyes, and her face is extremely charming. I am sorry if that is painful to you."

"It isn't, oddly. What does she do? Has she a job here?"

"Of course. She is an interpreter, employed by one of the largest banks. She was married once, a long time ago."

"And do you want to live with her?"

The car stopped abruptly, pulled to the side of the long,

straight, deserted road. Wasim turned to his wife, gripped her arm brutally.

"Do you have to be so calm about it? I can't stand it."

"What else should I be? And I shall just have to stand it."

They stared at one another in the darkness, Justine's quiet, reflective face exploring Wasim's, and there she saw the contortions of guilt and of self-seeking impatience; and the part of her that had fallen in love with him and played so frivolously shrivelled up, atrophied, and fell away. There was only a little pain, and then it was gone.

"Well," she said, treating him like the spoilt child the rest of her had been humouring for nearly eight years, "it seems to me that you should bring her to live with us. The apartment is plenty big enough for three."

"*What?* Have you gone out of your mind? She would never consent."

"And what else would you suggest?"

Wasim breathed hard. His face twisted. "I want a divorce from you."

Justine saw again, like a tableau beamed up in front of her, the supplicating, reaching hands.

"Oh no, I couldn't agree to that." Her voice trembled only somewhat.

"And why not? If I don't love you any more, if I openly tell you that I'm unfaithful several times a week, that I love another woman, that I don't want you to stay in my house – *why* then do you yourself not want a divorce? It is the civilised answer."

His wife, expressionless in profile, stared through the blurred windscreen at the unsympathetic night.

"It's quite simple, really," she said. "It's got nothing to do with love – that's irrelevant in most marriages, and it's certainly so in ours."

"I fail to understand you." Wasim, offended, spoke stiffly. Theirs had been a marriage of love, of mutual passion, hadn't it? A genuine affair of the heart, not one of those outdated marriages by arrangement. How degrading were her words! He began to feel the first seeds of hatred; impatient now -

"Just for God's sake tell me why you would want to stay with me?"

Justine turned to him, and her intelligent, tired face with its fading blank green eyes frightened him.

"I *like* being married to you," she said.

* * *

If that was the problem, thought Wasim wildly over the next few weeks as he wrestled with the difficult concepts of acceptance, forgiveness and forbearance, it was easily fixed.

I will make her *not* like being married to me! I will make her so heartily dislike it that she will come running to me, begging on her bloody ancient knees for a divorce. I will make her *loathe* being married to me. So his fevered notions ran on: for now he was utterly involved with Antoinette, anxious to be with her, to have her in his home. He began to practise small cruelties on Justine.

One day, when she was shopping on Casablanca's swankiest boulevards, Justine had taken the credit card that Wasim allowed her in his name. She had never been extravagant, having that enviable knack of picking up classic, low key items and dressing them up with stylish jewellery, well cut shoes; and he trusted her. Today she merely wanted new footwear, low heeled and comfortable for her slightly spreading feet. It was hot now that she spring had come with an early heat wave. Still the beggars lay in the streets, through the suffocating warmth of mid-

day and early afternoon, still the blackened hands plead-
ed, still the man without legs hauled himself along by the
elbows, scraping his metal hip plates along the pavement,
still the urchins ran cheerfully, unshod, though the souqs
had closed shop until the evening and the cafe bars sprin-
kled water on the sidewalks to freshen the place and deter
the flies. Mildly sickened by the odours wafted by the sudden heat, Justine scuttled into town.

She found just the shoes she wanted – foreign, expensive, hand-stitched leather – at Khalifa's boutique. Smiling, the assistant brought out the shoes in her size. Smiling, Justine tried them, smiling presented the credit card;
smiling, waited.

The assistant consulted the manager; frowned. Guttural Arabic mixed with bastard French, and Justine's smile
faded. With an unnerving flash of foresight she knew that -

"I'm afraid, Madame," said the manager, with regret,
for he liked this pretty, gentle lady and admired her excellent taste, "I am sorry to say that your husband has instructed this card not to be honoured."

"I see."

Justine paused, drew in her lips, making her mouth ser-
ried and old. The manager and his assistant regarded her
sadly, perceiving this, and murmured to themselves.

"Put the item by for me," said Justine, firmly. "I will
bring in the cash next week."

The manager observed the wide smile that restored her
beauty, and was glad.

But she did not. Could not. When she announced her
departure for Tangier, there to sail for Gibraltar, Touri first
flung a temper tantrum and then a bout of high fever, demanding that she stay and care for him.

"You are, after all, my *wife*," he said with malice in his
over bright eyes. And collapsed onto the pillows.

196

So Justine lost her shoes, the respect of Khalid and his assistant, and a week of her precious time, of her rapidly-ebbing life tide. She knew that she must be quick, must hurry now, or she would lose it all.

Wasim proved a trying patient. His fever was authentic, there was no doubt about that; how he had managed to summon it up remained a mystery. Justine knew only that if she crossed his will in any way, he would do it again. She fell into a fit of depression, but when Wasim was well and absenting himself as usual she took a grip upon herself and pursued what she had to do. Two batches of new stories were written up at speed, hurriedly checked and sent off to her agent in the far-away country that Touri hated, that chilly, colourless place where reason rules and fevered emotions and witchery don't stand a chance. The agent, seeing the need, replied post haste that she would certainly place these stories. *Am trying new publisher*, she said.

"All publishers are trying," murmured Justine to herself, with that ageing, wry, dry twist to her once-alluring mouth, "But just get my stories in, for goodness' sake, get them in."

And she willed herself to overlook the other, petty spites that Wasim inflicted on her, the items of Antoinette's that he would drop carelessly about the place: once a glove small enough to fit the hand of a child, a pearl earring, and even, finally and insultingly, a pair of briefs surely designed for the most vulgar kind of strip-tease. Justine was reminded that Wasim too was getting older, and old men's fancies were common knowledge. Then she allowed herself a faint, tight smile.

"Well," he said to her belligerently one day, "and how do you like your life now? Eh? Not very agreeable, is it, my dear? After all, you do not go out in the evenings any more, and it can't be very nice to be alone so much in the apartment."

"Oh, I don't know," said Justine with a tranquillity that made Wasim's skin itch. "I still like being married to you."

"You do? You must be crazy. Yes, that's it! I'll have you locked up for a mad woman. That'll be the end of it."

"I doubt it," said Justine, with a yawn of dismissal.

"You do, eh? Well, let me tell you I have a lot of influential friends, and it will be no trouble to find someone who will do as I want."

Justine said nothing, but only smiled again. Wasim looked into the depths of the green eyes, and sensed himself on shifting sands. He was not sure how, but his intuition told him that she might outwit him. That much closeness had come from this marriage. Perhaps it is the way all marriages run, when it comes down to it.

* * *

Antoinette came to the apartment. First for a visit, and then for a few days and then – well, it was inevitable, they all agreed, that she should stay. After all, they were cosmopolitans, this was twenty-first century Casablanca, not medieval Mecca. Of course they could do it.

And they did. Or at least, Justine and Antoinette managed the situation. In fact, they actively liked each other. It was strange, Justine reflected one warm afternoon as she listened to the sounds of Wasim and his mistress making love in the large, balconied master bedroom, it was most odd, but she had liked Antoinette on sight. The feeling appeared to have been returned. After all, there was a difference of some twenty-five years in their ages; she could have been Antoinette's mother.

Justine padded barefoot onto the balcony of her own

small room and looked down on the stillness that was Casablanca on a July afternoon. The streets below were mantled in summer dust, and already the trees had the dried-out dull green of the hot season, the withered leaves on their parched branches hanging stiff, like the arms of the man who sat in the dirt and sold old-fashioned hairpins, antique elastoplasts, garnered bits and pieces on the edge of the souq for a pitiful few centimes. The days of burning heat stretched across the landscape, lining up one by one on the shimmering horizon, relentlessly marching on the city from now until late September. Justine sighed. It was difficult to work in the summer and in this small space.

Sounds filtered from the master bedroom, distinctive to the act and particular to Wasim and Antoinette. It was always the same.

"My love, my darling, my little French bird!"

"Oh, you angel, oh Wasim, oh how I, oh!"

"I come, my beloved, I come like the moon on the desert, oh I come now!"

"Yes, come, my Wasim, oh come with me, my dearest!"

And so on, degenerating rather into formless noises thereafter.

The faintly pinched, wise mouth twitched as Justine recalled the story she had punched into her typewriter the previous day. She listened more carefully, putting her ear to the rough white wall of the balcony.

Of course, Antoinette was able to converse in English, for the girl was a linguist, a most accomplished one, and spoke several languages. This infuriated Wasim for the women – his women – would chatter away amiably together in a tongue of which he knew hardly a word. He hoped they were not talking about him.

Antoinette was also beautiful, that was true. She was

not as startlingly elegant or unusual as Justine had been in her day, but blonde and elfin, rather chic in the French way, with fine bones to the face. It was Antoinette that Wasim showed off at parties now, and it was for Antoinette that he received due compliments. It had to be said, however, that Antoinette had a rather large behind, and though sensual enough now it was the kind that would broaden and droop – well, if her life was to go the way of most women's. In her less generous moments, Justine hoped that it would.

She need not have worried. Antoinette, whilst happy to share the apartment with Justine, this older, no longer desirable woman who happened to be most kind to her, although she was moderately content with their arrangement, she also fiercely wanted Wasim for herself and for always. Antoinette had no two sides to her earthy, practical nature; no observing, calculating, appraising inner eye; she was openly, wholeheartedly, and unreservedly in love with Wasim and saw only one way of keeping him.

It was in early October that she announced her pregnancy.

"I am with child," she said proudly one morning, and staggered to the bathroom to be sick.

"My God! I don't believe her," said Wasim in horror, but the retching was unmistakable. His first wife had suffered terrible morning sickness with each of the pregnancies. He shuddered. "Well, she must get rid of it."

"Wasim!" Justine decided to be shocked. "That poor girl. How can you even think of such a thing?"

And she followed Antoinette to the shower-room, where she was so gentle in her ministrations and so comforting that Antoinette felt herself bound in the moment more to the wife than to the husband, and even in her nauseated state she pondered on the strangeness of it.

The next months continued in this manner. Sick as a dog each day, Antoinette was fattening round the middle while her face became drawn and sweaty. The blonde hair hung lank and tending to be greasy; her brown eyes dimmed in protest, as if they could not believe what parturition was doing to her, this simple act of nature. Justine, who had never carried a child, could only wonder at what she observed, and be thankful that she had been spared this misery so that her years with Touri had been peaceful and unspoiled.

Wasim reflected on this too. As the stricken Antoinette ritually heaved in the far bathroom to which she had been banished, he looked at Justine with fresh appreciation. Her motherly concern for the younger woman had given her new life, new vibrancy, and her eyes twinkled the greener, her skin bloomed and her hair shone. It was miraculous – but it was as if Justine was having the good pregnancy that she might have had in youth, whilst Antoinette endured a bad one. For women are sharply divided into those for whom child bearing is their best state, for whom nature might have designed this thing, and the others, who carry badly. Justine was the one, Antoinette the other.

Most certainly, Justine looked younger again – she even moved with that former fluidity of long-legged elegance that Wasim had so much adored. For a woman of fifty-seven, she was remarkable.

"We shall go to my uncle's party tonight, you and I," he said, and touched Justine on the hand.

Of course, Antoinette could not be left behind, but she went very much as the third leg of the handsome pair. She did her best, pulling her poor limp hair back into a velvet bow and rouging her cheeks; but the child within was growing rapidly, and against her stretched face and neck the ungainly bulge under the billowing dress looked ridiculous. Justine, on the other hand, sparked messages from the rekindled eyes, tossed her hennaed hair round her animated face, so that men who had ignored her for months began to move to her side.

"My goodness," whispered Omar in Wasim's ear. "I have to say, your wife looks absolutely fantastic! What have you been doing to her?"

"My boy," said Uncle Morad, "you have been hiding Justine from us this last year – and now I can see why. If I were only younger!"

Of the pale, wilting Antoinette they took little note, only chiding Wasim good naturedly.

"You should marry that poor creature," they said, "and make her look a bit better. She is ill because of her unfortunate situation. Get married, and she will become beautiful."

And Wasim chafed and inwardly raged that they seemed not to remember Antoinette's beauty before this cursed state. But perhaps they were right; perhaps her poor looks were something to do with being unhappy. Very well, then: he would marry her. After all, he could, under Muslim law, take another wife, three more if he wanted; and Justine, well, she was just there.

Rather more than just there, though, Wasim mused as he glanced across at the entrancing shape of his wife with the small group of men around her. How on earth had she done this to herself? Had she secretly visited some brilliant doctor, or a plastic surgeon, on her mysterious visits to the European mainland? Paid to have a curse put upon her rival, the pathetic, ailing Antoinette? Or was it just that he, Wasim, was nearing fifty at last and was able to see with the gaze of a more mature man? Was this something he had not seen, not recognised, so taken up had he been with his new love? Wasim's head swam with all these possibilities and the whisky they were drinking, and he shook it from side to side, confused and for a moment as dizzy and maudlin as his pregnant mistress.

To rid himself of these tiresome perplexities he took Justine to the big bed in the ornate double room that night. Antoinette he left to groan by herself and get over her heartburn in the smallest of the three guest rooms, at the other end of the apartment.

In the white light of a December moon he made love to his wife, who responded with such a warmth and such intimate ease that Wasim sobbed his gratification and off-loaded his guilt in the same instant.

"Justine," he said, looking deep into the shining silver-green eyes, "I have been unkind to you. Do you, can you–?"

But she laid a hand across his mouth and silenced him with her body. Antoinette, lying awake in her maidenly bedroom, listened to the noises that followed, and determined that she would have this child, and then another, and another. And perhaps –

Loudly, she burped, and smiled on the exhalation of gas.

Ignorant of these plans for his future, Wasim lost himself between his wife's milky thighs and thought of nothing.

The child was born in April, near the end of the month. It was a fine, attractive boy, very like Wasim. The father was enchanted with the baby and with himself, gathered all his relations to see this wonderful son (his previous wife had borne him two remarkably plain girls) and was generally nice to Antoinette. Justine he kept in his bed.

Sure enough, Antoinette blossomed and bloomed anew in the mothering period. Those sickly in the nine months of preparation often come into their own when the tender business of milking the child absorbs their days. (Even

Lady Macbeth admitted to this weakness.) She took on the look of a classic painting, rounded and healthy with bright wide brown eyes. The blonde hair regained its colour and texture, grew longer, astonishingly thick and luxuriant round her recovered face. Her breasts – not formerly of note – swelled with the engorging fluid. Above all, she was utterly happy. Wasim was drawn irresistibly to her, wanted frantically to share with his infant son the marvellous post-partum effects, and soon he insisted that Antoinette move back into the master suite and that the infant Riad – remarkably good, never waking in the night – should have a crib in there with them. Suspended in the limbo of new motherhood, Antoinette scarcely noticed these changes. Her new-born energy charged her days and nights with the passion of living, which she transferred effortlessly to Wasim's seeking body, his hungry soul. Like his small son, he fed off Antoinette's vitality. A time of milk and honey, milk and honey.

Justine, by contrast, seemed leached of colour and form. Those women who take to pregnancy sometimes decline after the birth, reducing to a less flattering weight, lose hair, fall into melancholy. By proxy, as it were, Justine echoed this pattern and also suffered that indefinable ennui that dulled her looks and her spirits. Hers was the small room again, the banishment, but from where she could hear not only the rapturous reunion of Wasim and Antoinette but also the joyful cooing and gurgling as they played with the precious son.

For Wasim, at last fifty, was finding fatherhood diverting. Antoinette made it easy for him, whereas the mother of his daughters had complained and found numberless reasons to be unwell and dissatisfied. Antoinette wisely shared her body and her good humour with him. He would marry her. His relatives were right; it was the proper thing.

But first, he wished after all to divorce Justine.

"I do not wish to be like the old time Muslims," he said with a gesture of disdain. "I shall have only one wife – and that will be my beautiful Antoinette – mother of my son," he added, as a final shot.

"But I do not want a divorce," said Justine steadily.

"Justine." Wasim put his hands on her shoulders, looked at her not unkindly. "We had again a brief time together, you and I. Let us part on that sweet memory. Now Antoinette is well, she is young, and she is very important to me. How can you live here as my wife?"

Justine shook her drab, roughened, brownish hair as a mule dusts off its coat.

"I *like* being married to you," she said.

The veins in Wasim's forehead stood out. The large dark eyes bulged.

"You really must be stupid! Very well, I shall go about getting a divorce in another way, one that does not require your consent."

In her deliberate manner, Justine removed the hands that were pleating the fine silk of her shirt. She recalled the hands of the blind and the forlorn on the streets outside; hands into which she had, lately, taken to dropping a few coins like talismans for her own good fortune.

"I would be careful, if I were you," she said. "You might make a fool of yourself."

And walked away to her little room, her exile, with the old typewriter and the sheets of paper covered in English.

* * *

Some weeks later, Wasim got an appointment to see the lawyer. There would be no problem, so far as he could see. After all, this was an Arab country, where women had fewer rights, and in any case he had enough money to pay for whatever he wanted done. Justine's protests would be irrelevant.

For a moment, the lawyer stared at him without speaking. Then he said that Wasim would have to go about this matter, how should he say, judiciously? One would have to be cautious, one must understand. He spoke of reputation, of honour, and a lot of other things that Wasim did not want to hear at this time. He stared at the older man indignantly.

"What do you mean? I have plenty of money, as you must now. I am of the Hassan family here."

"Yes, yes, that is true." There was a fiddling of papers, shifting of a paperweight. "But you see... Well, I would have thought you would have been aware... It is all over Casablanca."

"*What* is all over Casablanca?"

The lawyer pursed his yellowed lips, put his parchment fingertips together, adjusted his light jacket, looked at his client cautiously with his discoloured eyes. This reminded Wasim uncannily of Justine in one of her cryptic moods. He shifted uneasily in his chair.

"I ask you, tell me, just what are you talking about? What should I know about?"

A thin, discreet cough; a circling of the air with the old hands.

"Your wife... Justine. She has published two collections of stories. In English, originally, of course, but recently translated into French. Her publishers have placed them in the bookshops now, and I believe there might be some of them – what does one call it? – on line? Naturally the word has started getting around and everyone has wanted to read them."

"*And?*"

Wasim had a terrible premonition in his bowels. He never read fiction, dismissing it as lightweight, superficial, women's stuff.

"Well, it seems that these stories – I have only glanced at one or two, you understand, as the content is rather shocking for one so orthodox as I – but her stories, your wife's stories, well... they..."

"They *what?*"

Fury blazed in Wasim's eyes. He pushed himself forward aggressively at the old man, who spread his papery hands before him.

"Hassan, please, please! I am trying to explain to you. Your wife's stories, though purely fictional, of course, do yet mirror your own, how shall I put it, your very situation. They are most well written – so I am told – but they concern a man who is vain and – I am sorry to say this but selfish, and who, moreover, well, has a dishonourable attitude towards the women he loves and casts aside. I regret further to have to say that some have identified you with this man, the protagonist of several of the stories, and that he emerges as less than a decent character."

The stunned silence in the dusty office was punctuated only by Wasim's fierce out breaths as he contemplated this unwelcome information.

"You are saying that I am vain and selfish and dishonourable?"

"No, no, Hassan, not at all! As your family's solicitor, I know better than to assume anything of the kind, be assured of that. I am merely – well, yes, warning you that there are those people who, in ignorance, naturally, have seen in you some aspects of this despicable fictional character – only in certain aspects, that goes without saying... and that you might be thought of in this way if you... well, if you treat your wife and the mother of your son in any way that is less than kind."

"I see."

And in unconsciously echoing his wife's earlier words, Wasim did see, all too clearly. In other words, fashionable Casablanca was beginning to laugh at him. The stories had been read and were being passed around, these scurrilous and purely fabricated tales; people were watching and waiting for his next move. He recalled Justine's words, her calm, light cat's eyes in the senescent face; and he cursed, long and foully, and spat upon the lawyer's floor.

*   *   *

During the next few weeks, Wasim made arrangements to marry Antoinette. The wedding was a quiet affair, with no great extended three-day family party as was the custom; nevertheless a pleasant occasion, marred for Wasim only by the fact that Antoinette had insisted Justine be present. The two women had grown close, Justine taking on a sort of grandmotherly role in the care of the little boy; and now that she knew herself to be in safe harbour she put out her best rig again and coasted smoothly round Wasim and his profound high dudgeon. Once again she resurrected her hair. Her eyes brightened and deepened as she dandled the infant upon her still shapely knees, and a serenity enveloped her which was undeniably attractive, perhaps not in an urgent sexual way but in some more secret, hidden fashion like the seductive charms of Morocco itself.

They attended social evenings now as a threesome: middle-aged Wasim, a little less athletic and a tad wider round the waist, a quietly luminous Antoinette with her sheaf of primrose hair, and the tall, intriguing older wife with the bewitching eyes. Wasim graciously accepted compliments on both of them.

"Your little wife – so very French! She is charming, Wasim."

"Thank you."

"Your older wife – still so regal, so marvellously slender! You are indeed doubly lucky, Hassan."

"Thank you."

"With two such women in the house, and a fine son, how could a man be discontented with his lot?"

How indeed? Wasim was certainly not unhappy. Justine occasionally found herself under her needy husband in the wide marital bed, though more often it was Antoinette, of course. She too was content. She had her freedom and she had Wasim ,she was still writing (and quite wealthy in her own right, though Wasim was unwilling to acknowledge any of her stories or the existence of any money from them) and she had a surrogate grandson whom she adored. She also adored Antoinette, who had become like a daughter, for she was gentle, clever and affectionate. The two would sit for hours and chat, and walk with little Riad, taking a plump baby hand each, and laugh together in the sun.

"Are you really going to publish more stories about us?" asked Antoinette one day.

"Oh, I don't know. I might. I don't need the money, of course, but if I think the time is right, then yes, I will."

Antoinette regarded her sharply, opened her mouth, but said nothing.

Three months later she was pregnant once more. Like the first, it was a sickly, uncomfortable gestation. Riad was less than two years old, and Justine took over much of the care of him. This time she did not bloom as much herself; she was, after all, soon to be sixty. Wasim tore his hair and vowed to become a recluse, a celibate. Antoinette laughed at him and as usual went to be sick.

This second child was born after a short and easy labour: another son, named Morad after Wasim's uncle, who was delighted. Wasim was happy, but less euphoric. Antoinette was as beautiful in motherhood as ever, but he was slowing down. He wanted quiet strolls, tranquil adult dinners, not dribbling infants and baby food on the floor. However, despite the grumbles, they got through this difficult time and all was well, if not quite, not exactly as before.

Antoinette's third child was born three years later; Wasim swore he did not know how this had happened, as he had insisted that Antoinette take the pill and did not want to hear about statistical possibilities of failure even in this supposedly surefire method. This time Antoinette was very ill, and it was for whatever reason of fate a tricky birth. The child was a girl, of no consequence to Wasim but a wonder, a miracle and a source of immense joy to Antoinette and also to Justine, though with her hands full looking after Riad and Morad, she insisted on getting in some paid help. She too was tired, and could no longer summon up those rejuvenating vibrations.

"I shall cut off all my parts," said Wasim in a rage as he took his cursory look at the tiny, crumpled infant girl. "I have no more use for them."

And later, when he observed how the three children, the two wives and the nursemaid had taken over his apartment, he took to staying out often and late. This suited everyone admirably.

One evening, Wasim returned rather earlier than usual – about nine o'clock – in a fine temper. His formerly well-favoured face was heavy and sullen, and Antoinette wondered mildly as she moved her nuzzling daughter from one swollen breast to the other why she had once found him so attractive. Justine had long since ceased to ponder such a pointless question.

"I want a divorce," said their husband. "From both of you."

The women looked at each other, and raised their eyebrows, as mothers do over the heads of their unruly children at play. Antoinette pushed back her untidy, straggling hair. Wasim regarded them contemptuously.

"Look at the pair of you," he said. "Old women, both of you, and not even an attempt to look well. How can I be seen with you?"

"Have you got another woman?" asked Antoinette, dabbing her little girl's chin clean of surplus milk.

Wasim looked from one pair of placid eyes to the other and back again, and suddenly felt himself trapped between the brown gaze and the green as is a rabbit between hunters' guns. His shoulders sagged.

"Yes."

Justine and Antoinette glanced at each other again in that maddeningly complicit way. Each nodded.

"In that case, bring her to live here," they said.

Wasim's fist banged down onto the table, making the baby startle in her mother's arms, whimpering as she lost the nipple.

"I want a divorce, you stupid bitches!"

Without a word, Justine went to her cramped work room, brought out the tell-tale sheets of paper densely typed in English. Wasim, with dread in his mind and that unpleasant sensation in his lower regions, thought he knew what these were. His wife handed them to him, but he backed away. There, in her pale green eyes, he saw himself, a minuscule upside-down reflection like the hanged man.

"You will not agree to a divorce?"

Antoinette and Justine, in perfect unison, shook their heads.

"But why in heaven's name not?" Wasim asked, in desperation. He could not move this new girl into the apartment; she would never agree, not this one. And he was too old, too weary, he could not face a harem, not at his age. "Why will you not have a divorce? I would promise to keep you well and you could all live together. So long as I could see my sons."

The synchronised heads shook again, slowly, like some nightmare puppet show.

"You don't understand, do you?" asked Antoinette, with the patience of an indulgent parent.

"No, I don't." Wasim fretted about the room. "I am just your dumb old husband, I get that, but would one of you be good enough to explain?"

"Poor old Wasim." Justine moved to cosset him.

Her husband wrenched his arm away viciously, bared his fine teeth in the manner of a captured savage who speaks no language but his own. His breath came unevenly, in quite the manner of the romantic hero; but love, romance and all that goes with it was far from him at this instant. Wasim was cornered, and by instinct he knew it.

"Spare me pity! Just give me one reason, something simple that even I, your stupid and yes, *old* husband, can grasp, why neither of you wants to end this farce of a situation. Eh? Enlighten me."

The steady, kind brown eyes of his French wife and the faded but humorous eyes of his American wife met in a telepathic flash; and then they turned their awful stare upon him. As one woman, they answered.

"Dear, darling Wasim," they murmured. "You still can't take it in, can you?"

"Take what in?" roared Wasim. "For the sake of Allah, don't speak in riddles. *Tell me what precisely it is that I don't understand."*

Two pairs of shoulders shrugged; two pairs of eyebrows lifted. Far below in the humid street the beggars counted their meagre haul and shuffled and dragged themselves to the hidden places where they spent their nights. The grilles clanged on the fronts of the pavement cafes and the shops served their last customers with groceries and mint tea. All hung in the motionless hiatus when the busy evening slips swiftly into night; and then the final muezzin call of the day sent forth its piercing metallic cry through the boulevards. Justine let out her breath. Antoinette sighed. In perfect harmony Wasim's wives softly dropped their thunderbolt of doom.

"Dearest Wasim," they said, "we *like* being married."

Lightning Source UK Ltd.
Milton Keynes UK
UKOW06f1422221017
311457UK00004B/57/P